Wilhelmina and the Willamette Wig Factory

Whitney Dineen

Published in the United States by Kissing Frogs Publications
an imprint of Thirty-Three Partners Publishing.

Library of Congress
Cataloguing-In-Publication Data
Dineen, Whitney
Wilhelmina and the Willamette Wig Factory:
a novel/ Whitney Dineen

ISBN-13: 978-1497431942

First Edition

From the Author

When I was in the first grade, the Chicago public school system sent my parents a letter telling them that due to test results, I was slated to be taken out of regular classes and placed into the special ed. program. My parents requested a meeting and challenged these findings. They did not take this pronouncement lightly. They had me retested by specialists and learned that I was not slow, rather I had a visual comprehension learning disability. What does this mean? It means that while I *could* read, I had zero comprehension of what I read. The specialists assured my parents that chances were very high I would begin to outgrow this disorder in my early teens.

Why am I telling you this? I'm sharing for two reasons. 1.) We all learn differently, all of us. You should never be embarrassed if you don't understand something. Talk to your parents, talk to your teachers and let them help you find the way you learn the best.

2.) Shame. As a kid, it can be difficult trying to figure out where you fit. You don't want to be different. You want to be like your friends. It is easy to feel shame and want to hide your problems.

When I was growing up, I never read for pleasure. I never read the classics that all kids should read. I felt humiliated by the fact that I didn't remember what I was reading, so I just didn't do it. When I was in junior high school, as predicted, I began to outgrow my disability and a new world opened up for me. By the time I was a junior in high school, I was in the honors program. While sitting in the library doing my homework, I used to look around in awe and think what an amazing accomplishment it must be to write a book. Thousands upon thousands have written books. I used to think that if all of those other people could do it, maybe one day I could too.

A learning disability is a funny thing. Years of feeling inferior to your classmates undermines your self-esteem. It makes you feel unsure of your chances at success. It took me until the middle of my life to believe in myself enough to give writing a chance. This is my third book. What I want you to take away from this is that you can accomplish any dream no matter how farfetched you think it is. Believe in yourself, always. If you are having trouble in any area in school or life, share that trouble with a trusted adult. Let others help you. Life in not a solo journey, we share it with others.

I would like to thank my parents, Libby and Reiner Bohlen, for always believing in me and encouraging me to become the best I could be. I would also like to thank the many teachers and authors who have inspired me on my journey.

Lots of love and appreciation to Wendy Gordon and all the great folks at The Albany Historic Carousel & Museum!

*This book is dedicated to my beautiful daughters,
Anna and Faith.
May your lives be full of adventure!*

Mason, the seventh and eight grades were in their own building and Willy couldn't wait to go to the junior high, directly across the street from the high school.

But here in the Willamette Valley, the sixth, seventh and eighth grades shared a building. Being new, she was sure everyone would think she was a sixth-grader. Red hair, freckles, unfortunately named and mistaken for a sixth-grader? Life couldn't possibly be any worse!

Emma Jean Snodgrass watched her daughter mope on the front stoop. She felt really bad for her. A move was hard at any age, but eleven she thought, was a particularly difficult time in a girl's life. Not quite a child and not quite a teen, those tween years were a killer. She remembered all too well. Maybe she would take Willy to downtown Monteith and get her some new play clothes for the summer. That ought to cheer her up. When Emma Jean suggested the outing to Willy, she was greeted with, "Geez Mom, I'm almost twelve. We don't call them play clothes anymore."

"Okay dear, let me rephrase. Would you care to go shopping with your thoroughly ignorant, un-hip mom and buy some cool new summer threads?"

Willy rolled her eyes, "Sure, why not. It's not like I have any friends to hang out with."

So off they went, mother and daughter on an

expedition to make life better through shopping. The movers continued to move and John Snodgrass, Willy's dad, continued to direct the action. Wendell ran around the yard with his new friends screaming like a herd of banshees, and life in the Willamette Valley was now a reality.

On the drive through town, Willy realized two things. First off, Monteith wasn't that different from Mason. Both towns were pretty small, both had a bunch of churches, a park with a swimming pool and the roads on both Main Streets were made of brick, from back in the horse and buggy days. Just as she was starting to feel a little at home, Willy thought about the second thing. As familiar as the town looked, she didn't know a soul in it.

It was like an episode of that old show her grandparents loved, *The Twilight Zone*. Everything was the same, but totally different. "Doo doo doo doo," she heard the show's theme song running through her head and she imagined a funny looking man in a dark suit walking out from behind a building saying, "You have now entered The Twilight Zone."

Willy's mom parked their mini-van on the street right in front of a store called The Glad Bag. The store looked pretty cool with a collection of low slung jeans in the window, belly shirts and lots of fun jewelry. Willy started to think the outing wasn't going to be so bad. When they walked in, a blast of cold air hit them and ever so slightly cooled her bad mood. A radically dressed teenager introduced herself as Charlene and told them that if they needed any direction with sizes and the like, she would be happy to help. Just when they started toward a rack of denim, Charlene looked Willy up and down and declared, "Hey Red, that is some of the coolest looking hair I've ever seen. Is that your real color or do you dye it?"

Shocked and pleased by the attention, Willy fibbed, "It's a rinse. I'm really a blonde."

Emma Jean looked at her daughter like she had grown a second head, but kept quiet and watched as her tween and this wild teenager continued their dialogue.

"No way! That is soooo cool! I love to do stuff with my hair. I just dyed my sister's hair blue with blueberry Jello and it's totally radical. Tommy's about your age. What are you, twelve?"

Willy answered, "I'll be twelve in August. I'm going into the seventh-grade in September."

Charlene brightened, "Then you have to know Tommy. She's going to be in the seventh-grade too."

"Well," Willy explained, "we just moved here from Illinois. I don't know anybody, yet."

Charlene started to refold some sweaters and said,

"Listen Red, you gotta meet Tommy. She is one of the coolest kids in the junior high. She knows all the ins and outs and she'll give you the scoop on the Monteith social scene. Where do you live?"

Willy looked at her mom and answered, "We live on Carousel Lane, but I don't remember the house number."

Emma Jean cut in, "We live at number 231. It's the two story white Victorian with the wrap around porch."

Charlene interrupted with a, "NO WAY! We live at 238 Carousel! Well, that settles it. I'm gonna have Tommy come over this afternoon to introduce herself. You guys will hit it off like a train on fire!"

All of a sudden, Willy felt like there might be hope for her in Monteith, Oregon. She and her mom spent the next forty-five minutes shopping for summer clothes and in the end she took home a new hot pink bikini, two pairs of cropped pants, a halter top and even a fake belly button ring. It was the belly button ring that made her realize her mom felt bad about the move. Had they still lived in Mason, she would have never approved that purchase.

Wilhelmina Rhonda Snodgrass started to think that there may, just may, be a light at the end of the tunnel. With any luck, that light might not be an oncoming train.

Wendell

Willy had to admit as far as little brothers went, Wendell was not the very worst she could have wound up with. As a matter of fact, her friend Ellie McDonald had that honor. Ellie's brother, Jimbo, always looked like he had rolled through mud, jam and worms. He was filthy and his nose ran. It was a combination so nauseating it was hard to look at him without losing your lunch. Jimbo and Wendell had been in the same class at Mason Elementary until the second grade when the Ford County school board invited Jimbo back to repeat the grade the following year. The boys were devastated that they wouldn't be in the same class anymore and vowed to keep their friendship alive even though they would now reside on different floors of the elementary school. Like true boys, a little obstacle like flunking a grade made no difference in their friendship. Willy was a little in awe of that because had she flunked out, she couldn't have held her head up in public, not without a disguise, a new name and a fake accent anyway. But she figured boys just had different priorities.

Wendell James Snodgrass became a member of the family during a particularly nasty spring storm in April. This made him almost three-and-one-half years younger than Willy. Willy didn't fully remember what life was like before Wendell, but she liked to think it was pretty wonderful. The family photo album held an array of pictures of Willy sticking out her tongue at her baby brother. In one frame, she was trying to sit on him and then there's her favorite shot of all. In that picture, she was holding Wendell and was just about to drop him on the floor when her mom screamed and blurred right through the photo. It was a live action shot!

For the first two-and-a-half years of Wendell's young life, Willy couldn't be bothered with him. But in the fall of her sixth year, she remembered how an eight year old neighbor boy named Duke Dunkin, began teasing her brother by calling him "Wendy wet pants." For whatever reason, Willy took grave offense at this taunting and marched right over to Duke and planted her fist square on his nose. Once that task was accomplished, she kicked him in the shin for good measure. No one was going to call her brother Wendy. What kind of parents did they have anyway that would name their daughter Willy and their son Wendy? Were they trying to get them beat up? Had they no foresight at all? It was the Duke Dunkin incident that brought out the protective instincts in Willy. From that day forward, no one dared call her brother Wendy and if anyone was going to taunt him, it would be her.

When Wendell found out about the move to Oregon, he was actually excited. He was sad to leave his best friends, Jimbo and Linc behind, but what the heck, he was moving to Oregon. Wendell was convinced that living in Oregon would be like living in an old western movie. He dug his cowboy hat, spurs, and toy six-shooter out of his toy box in the basement. He figured he'd be required by Oregon law to wear them every day. He did wear them every day too, until they actually moved. Yet when Wendell saw what the Willamette Valley really looked like, he wasn't even disappointed. He just put his western gear back in the toy box and resumed life as normal. Could nothing upset this boy? It bugged Willy to no end that her little brother was having such an easy time starting over.

On the drive from Mason to Monteith, after long hours in the back of the mini-van, Willy finally demanded, "Wendell, what is *wrong* with you? Doesn't it bother you at all that you're leaving your home and friends behind? Doesn't it bother you that you might never see Jimbo again? Do you even think about how awful that's going to be?" She was trying hard to get Wendell to face up to reality. She realized she was being a little mean but she wasn't quite sure he got it. Did he think this was some sort of vacation that he would get to go home afterwards?

Wendell's answer surprised her a bit. He looked at his sister long and hard before replying, "You know Willy, I'll miss Jimbo a bunch. I know I probably won't ever see him again, but he's not my family and he's not my home. You and mom and dad are my family and home is wherever you guys are."

Willy was taken aback by such a grown up statement coming out of the mouth of her eight-year-old brother. It made her feel protective of him all over again. Geez, just when she got comfortable hating him, he had to come up with something sweet and mushy. Against her will, she realized that he wasn't the worst little brother she could have wound up with. This stupid move to Oregon was getting more and more complicated by the second.

Willy had had no idea what was in store for her next.

The Parents

To Willy and Wendell, Emma Jean and John Snodgrass were totally old. They were in their thirties after all. Just imagine, after that they'd be in their forties! They met when they were college freshmen at the University of Illinois and got married during their junior year. It was John, their dad, who wanted to move to Mason after graduation. He grew up in the neighboring town of Marvin and always dreamed of living in Mason. He figured if he couldn't have grown up there himself, it was the best home he could give his future children. Marvin was a town of only four-hundred people and Mason was the closest big city to them with a thriving population of almost four thousand.

Emma Jean was thrilled to move to Mason after graduation. She grew up in Iowa, and Illinois and Iowa were so similar it was like she never left home. The day she and John moved into their first little home, she cried tears of joy. Their tiny starter-house on Bell St. was made up of two little bedrooms, one bathroom, a kitchen and a front room. But to Emma Jean, it was a mansion because it was all theirs.

John got a job at the John Deere factory right out of college. He was going to work in sales. It was the perfect job for him because everyday he got to drive out to all those beautiful farms and talk to farmers he'd known all his life.

Emma Jean had a hard time finding a job in Mason because her degree was in nineteenth-century art, with a minor in pottery. There wasn't much of a calling for that in central Illinois so she got herself a job at the IGA checking groceries. She thought it was the perfect job for someone just moving to a new town because she got to meet everyone as they were checking out. Not only did she make several friends that way but she found out all about the town. She also discovered who wasn't eating well-balanced meals by the kind of groceries they bought. For instance, was it any wonder Louella Finley was so hefty? She complained about it every time she checked out in Emma Jean's aisle.

"I'm telling you Emma Jean, I don't know how you stay so trim. No matter what diet I go on, I just can't seem to lose any weight. I think there's a defective gene in my family."

It was all Emma Jean could do not to point out to Mrs. Finley that Ho Ho's, Nutter Butters, and Cheetos weren't exactly diet food. But she just smiled and told her that she looked great. After all, it wasn't her place to point out Mrs. Finley's dietary deficiencies to her.

After Emma Jean and John had lived in Mason for two years, they thought life couldn't get any better. Then they found out Emma Jean was pregnant with Willy and life did get better. The couple spent all their free time turning the spare bedroom into a nursery. They painted it a bright sunny yellow, put up white gauzy curtains and a teddy bear border. When they came home from the hospital with their new baby girl, they were sure that Wilhelmina Rhonda Snodgrass was going to be the first woman president of the United States. Never once did it occur to them that her name was anything but beautiful.

Life for the Snodgrass family continued on in easy routine for the next few years. Emma Jean quit the IGA after Willy was born. Three years later baby Wendell arrived. They bought a bigger house across town to fit their growing family and the days came and went in blissful harmony. That is until John came home with his announcement. "Honey, you'll never believe the good news I got at work today!"

After a few attempts, Emma Jean finally sighed, "John, you had better just tell me because I *am* never going to guess."

With a huge grin on his face, he told her, "The district manager came into my office today and asked me if I'd ever considered moving to Oregon."

Emma Jean started to laugh, "Oh John, that's funny. Oregon? Imagine, why would we ever want to leave Mason? What did he say when you told him you didn't want to move?"

John was a little stunned by his wife's response and murmured, "Honey, you'd better sit down."

Emma Jean looked right into her husband's eyes and not so much sat down as fell down. Her knees actually buckled. Luckily she landed in a chair. In a panic, she asked, "What did you tell him, John?"

"Well, I told him that for the right promotion, we'd love to move to Oregon."

Emma Jean turned a very odd shade of pale and asked, "Did he offer you the right promotion, John?"

"He sure did, honey, and guess what? My new job starts in six weeks. So the way I figure it, as soon as the kids are out of school, we'll pack up and start our new life in Monteith, Oregon!"

This is how the Snodgrass family left Mason. The men in the family were more excited than Christmas morning and the women, well let's just say, they weren't quite as thrilled. Emma Jean packed the house, said goodbye to her friends and tried to make the children believe this was the best thing to ever happen to them. Wendell believed her. Willy did not.

Tommy

When Willy and her mom got home from The Glad Bag, she jumped out of the car almost before it stopped. She definitely had a new lease on life after learning there was a girl her age living right down the street. Willy ran past her dad who was sipping an iced-tea on the porch and flew through the front door of her new house. She didn't slow down one bit when she heard her mom yell, "Wilhelmina Rhonda Snodgrass, slow down right this minute before you break your neck!" She ran right past her brother, Wendell, jumped over a box in the living room and tore up the steps to her new bedroom. Once she saw all her old furniture in her new room, she realized it kind of felt like home after all.

Willy spent the next two hours unpacking her clothes and hanging up her shirts, pants and dresses. She put her socks and undies in the same drawers she had them in at her house in Mason. She unpacked all her knick-knacks and put them where they belonged on her dresser top. She found the box containing her bedding and made up her bed. Then she put her three favorite stuffed animals from childhood on the bed, not because she still played with them, but because they reminded her of her old room. After all that was done, Willy was worn out. She lay down on the bed to take a little rest and to think about what her friends at home were probably up to.

Bes and Ellie had most likely been at the swimming pool all day because tomorrow was swim team try-outs. Bes was great at the breast-stroke and was sure to win every meet in their age division. Ellie didn't swim any stroke very well but felt that the swim team was a terrific social outlet. Plus, she was totally in love with Ryan James, who was a year older than they were and he had been on the summer swim team for years. It was Ellie's only real chance to get him to notice her, since they were in different grades and all.

Willy was getting herself good and depressed thinking about home. She decided to get up and finish her unpacking. As she looked out the window next to her closet, she saw a girl with spikey blue hair and red sunglasses come up their driveway. "Wow," she thought, "That is some scary fashion statement!" She remembered that Charlene mentioned her sister Tommy had blue hair, just as the doorbell rang.

Still feeling lonely for her friends, Willy went downstairs to answer the door, only Wendell had beat her to it. She got there in time to hear him say, "What happened to your hair? Yuck!"

Tommy gave Wendell the once over and said, "Guess what twerp? I'm not here to see you, so get lost."

Willy decided then and there, that despite her startling appearance, she was going to be friends with this Tommy girl. She told Wendell to beat it and then introduced herself. "Hi, I'm Willy Snodgrass. I bet you're Charlene's sister, Tommy."

Tommy smiled "You got it, sister. Welcome to Carousel Lane!"

"Thanks. You wanna come in? We can go up to my room. It's almost all unpacked."

Tommy answered, "Cool, but first, I promised to give your mom a message from my mom."

The girls went to the kitchen where they found Willy's mom stringing beans for dinner. Willy said, "Hey Mom, Tommy from down the road is here and she wants to tell you something."

Willy's mom turned around and jumped back at the appearance of the blue-haired girl standing in the kitchen. "Hello, Tommy. Welcome to our home."

Tommy noticed her reaction and smiled, "Hey, Mrs. Snodgrass. My mom wanted me to tell you she's making you some cookies. She's going to bring them over later. Also, she wanted me to assure you I'm not a juvenile-delinquent, you know with the blue hair and all. I'm just learning to express my individuality." She added, "Plus, it totally washes out. It's only Jello. So anyway, welcome to Monteith!"

Emma Jean smiled at the unique looking girl in her kitchen, "Thank you, Tommy. I'm looking forward to meeting your mom and I think you are doing a marvelous job expressing your individuality."

Willy added, "Mom, we're going to go up to my room now, so when those cookies get here, maybe you can let us know?"

The girls went up the back steps to Willy's bedroom which was located on the second floor. One of the things she liked best about their new house was that there were two sets of stairs. One started in the living room and the other in the kitchen. They met up on a landing, and from there it was only 15 steps to the second floor.

When the girls got to Willy's bedroom, Tommy confided, "You know, up until now, I've been the only one in my class with a boy's name. What does Willy stand for anyway, Wilma?"

Willy sighed dramatically. "Something much worse than Wilma, I'm afraid. It's not like my parents are demented or anything, but, well, I was named after my grandmother." She hurried to add, "Who's a totally cool lady, by the way. It was her parents who were cruel naming her what they did."

Tommy cut in, "Are you going to tell me or not? If it makes you feel any better, no matter what your name is, mine is worse by a mile." She bemoaned, "I was named after my grandmother, too, and her parents must have been drinking when they named her. So, tell me already, what's your real name?"

Willy smiled, thinking there was no way Tommy's name could be worse, but she decided if Tommy could be out in public with blue hair, maybe she was an open-minded sort of girl and wouldn't judge her too harshly.

"Okay, here goes. My full name is Wilhelmina Rhonda Snodgrass."

Tommy started laughing and exclaimed, "That *is* ghastly!"

When she saw the crestfallen look on Willy's face she added, "But mine is still worse. Ready? The name my parents saddled me with is Thomasina Franchesca Andretti. Feel any better?"

Willy looked absolutely stunned and replied, "Actually, I do. That's a horrible name!"

With this shared confidence, the two girls bestowed a truly radiant smile upon each other and a spectacular new friendship was born.

The Willamette Valley

The first Saturday after the Snodgrass family moved to Oregon, Willy and Tommy laid on their backs in the grass in the Snodgrass's back yard and tried to figure out what all the shapes in the clouds really were. Tommy was wearing bib-overalls and a sea foam green T-shirt. Oddly, her hair kind of matched her shirt. When Willy asked what happened, Tommy told her that the blueberry Jello didn't wash out all the way. So with her naturally blonde hair and the blueberry residue, the result was this aqua-green. Willy felt bad for her. The overall effect was that Tommy looked seasick and was about to hurl.

Willy pointed to the sky and exclaimed rather excitedly, "Tommy look, that cloud looks just like a dolphin."

"No way. Look closer. It looks more like Frankenstein. See the flat head and the bolt coming out of the neck?"

Willy eyed her friend oddly, "Nooooooo, I don't see a bolt coming out of a neck. I don't see a neck."

Tommy rolled her eyes, "You're not using your imagination."

After several minutes of eyeing the shape-shifting clouds Willy demanded, "Tommy, tell me about the Willamette Valley. Have you lived here your whole life? And where did they come up with a name like Monteith, anyway?"

Tommy considered her friend's questions a moment before she answered, "The town was named after two brothers with the last name of Monteith, who settled here back in the eighteen hundreds. We moved here when I was five. I was born on Long Island, New York." She continued, "My dad always wanted to be a cowboy, so when I was four and Charlene was nine, he planned this family vacation for us to visit a dude ranch in Scio." She explained, "Scio is northeast of here. So anyway, while we were there, my dad hears about the Willamette Valley Rodeo. That's a rodeo that takes place here every June. At the rodeo my dad starts talking to this old guy, Jake Lamour, and finds out that Jake owns the hardware store in Monteith, but he wants to sell out so he can retire. So what do you think my dad does? My dad, who by the way, was a New York City cop at the time?"

Willy was listening so intently to her new friend she didn't realize Tommy was waiting for an answer. Finally, she answers, "What? What did your dad do?"

"He bought the flippen' hardware store! Up until six-and-a-half years ago my dad didn't even know what a Phillips head screw driver was."

Willy, who still didn't know what a Phillips head screw driver was, asked, "So that was it? You just moved here with no warning?" She lamented, "Man, it's kind of like what my parents did to me. One day they just sat us down and said, 'your dad got a promotion and we're moving to Oregon.' What's with parents, anyway? Don't they realize that they're messing with lives here?"

"Hey Wilma," Tommy teased, "I was only five, so it really wasn't a big deal for me. Plus, think about it, if you'd never moved here, how would you have met my fabulous self?"

Willy laughed, "Okay, Tommy, let's say you're worth uprooting my whole life for. What else is there to know about the Willamette Valley? Were there ever any Wild West gun battles here? Was Jesse James ever held in the Monteith jail? Is this where the Lone Ranger met Tonto? Anything?"

Tommy put her finger to her lips as if in deep thought and said, "Actually, there is something. Edna May Tilman, who lives three blocks over, won the blue ribbon for her pickled beets four years running at the state fair in Salem."

Willy threw a handful of grass right at Tommy for the smart-aleck answer. Pickled beets were not exactly the thing legends were made of.

Tommy brushed off the grass, "Come on. Let's walk around town. The best way for you to get to know Monteith is to see it up close and personal."

The girls went into the house and told Willy's mom what they were up to. After promising to be back by five-thirty to help with dinner, they were on their way. They walked up Carousel Lane, took a left on Trout St. and then went straight down to First. First Street in Monteith, Oregon had two pharmacies, four clothing stores, The Glad Bag, Mr. Andretti's hardware store, The Hair Hutch, five restaurants, four antique shops, a bank, dance studio and an old time five-and-dime. First Street didn't take that long to cover. Willy did find out that if she ever wanted to have her hair cut, she should have Sheila McNut at The Hair Hutch do it. Sheila was the only beautician in town under the age of twenty-five and therefore had her finger on the very pulse of central Oregon's pre-teen hair fashions.

Once the girls covered First Street, they headed over to Church Street. Church was well-named as the girls passed four different ones in three blocks. From

Church, they detoured to Walnut. Walnut was a pretty little street with big shade trees running up and down both sides. To Willy, it seemed like the perfect place for grandmothers to live. The houses were all old Victorians that had been restored. There were flower gardens everywhere and she could swear she smelled the aroma of chocolate chip cookies wafting in the breeze.

Willy exclaimed, "I love this street! I wish my parents bought a house here."

"Don't I know it? One of my favorite people in the whole world lives here. Her name's Mrs. Carbunkle."

Willy laughed, "For real? Carbunkle?"

Tommy jabbed her new friend in the ribs, "Yes, Carbunkle." Smiling she continued, "Not really a name that Wilhelmina Rhonda and Thomasina Franchesca should make fun of, huh?"

"Oh gosh, you're right, but Carbunkle? It sounds like something that grows on old people's feet, doesn't it?"

Tommy gave up and giggled, "It does. Hey, I bet that chocolate chip cookie smell is coming from Mrs. C.'s house. Wanna meet her?"

The answer to that question was a no brainer so the girls walked the two blocks to an enchanting Victorian house with a porch swing and a mailbox that looked like a bird house. The name on the mailbox was Georgianna Carbunkle. The smell of cookies was stronger than ever and both girls realized this was indeed the house where the wonderful scent came from. With big smiles on their faces and drool at their mouths, they walked up to the front door and rang the bell. The bell didn't go ding-dong or buzz, but it chirped like a tree full of birds. After they "rang" for the second time, they heard a voice holler out, "Kindly hold your horses. I'll be there when I get there." Moments later, a rather round old lady in a red apron came to the door. Her hair was pulled back in a bun and she had a huge smile on her face.

"Well here I am and look who it is! My good friend Thomasina has stopped by and she's brought a friend. Would you two lovely ladies like to come in for some cookies?"

Tommy answered, "We'd love to Mrs. C." Then she introduced, "This is my new friend, Willy. She just moved in down the street from me."

Mrs. Carbunkle turned to Willy with a smile and asked, "Willy? Dear, I can't call you that. What is Willy short for, Wilhelmina?"

Willy was surprised that Mrs. Carbunkle guessed, "Yes it is, but how did you know?"

Mrs. C. gave her a warm smile and answered,

"Because I love the name Wilhelmina and would have given my daughter that very same name, if I ever had one, that is."

Willy was relieved that Mrs. C. never had a daughter to inflict that name on, but was still a little flattered someone outside her family liked it so much. The girls went into Mrs. C.'s front room, which she called the parlor. They devoured their cookies and milk and had an all-in-all wonderful time. Willy asked her if she had lived in Monteith her whole life and found out that she had. She asked Mrs. Carbunkle what she used to be when she was young. Was she a cowgirl, a mom, a teacher? Mrs. C. loved to talk about herself and Moneith, so she told the girls that although she was the mother of four boys, she was also the owner and operator of the once famous Willamette Wig Factory.

Tommy was shocked by this news, "The Willamette Wig Factory? I've never heard of it and I've lived here for almost seven years. Mrs. C., are you making this up?"

Georgianna Carbunkle assured Tommy she was not making it up. If the girls were to walk down Walnut to the end and take a left into the alley, they would come upon the entrance to the old shop. Tommy knew the building Mrs. C. was talking about, but thought it was just some old abandoned factory.

Her elderly friend assured her that's exactly what it was, an old abandoned factory; her family's old abandoned factory. She explained it was a working business from 1889 until 1985, when she closed up shop. The girls were just warming to this new topic when they heard the cuckoo clock chirp out five times.

Unhappily, Willy said, "Mrs. Carbunkle, I would love to hear more about the factory, but my mom's expecting us home in a half-hour. If we don't leave now, we'll be late. Can we come back and find out more about it another day?"

"Oh, absolutely. Wilhelmina dear, you and Thomasina are always welcome. Let me give you some cookies to take home."

Mrs. C. wrapped up a basket full of cookies and the whole way home the two girls talked about the wig factory. Imagine, a mysterious factory, right there in Monteith!

The Andrettis

The Andrettis were probably the coolest and oddest family that Willy had ever met. Mr. Andretti was a great big tank of a man. He was at least six feet, five inches tall, which made him seem totally scary at first. Willy knew he used to be a New York City cop, so she was automatically a little nervous to meet him. It wasn't until he smiled that she realized he was just a big teddy bear. He had the most wonderful smile and it made him look just like a kid.

Mrs. Andretti, on the other hand, was a knockout! There is just no other way to describe her. She was tall, blonde, blue-eyed, and she had the figure of a supermodel. It turns out that Mrs. Andretti *was* a model before she married Mr. Andretti. Willy couldn't imagine a more glamorous life than being a model in New York City.

Tommy told Willy that her parents met while her mom was getting mugged in the subway. Some junkie was trying to steal her purse and while she was putting up a good fight, she slipped and fell, losing hold of the strap. Dominic Andretti saw what was happening and sprinted after the guy. The mugger took one look at Dom, dropped the purse and ran for his life. As much as Dom wanted to go after the thief, he needed to make sure the gorgeous blonde was okay. So he grabbed the handbag and went back to the subway to find her. When Ginger saw him, she started to yell, "Did you get him? I hope you knocked him into next week! Well?" she demanded, "Quit standing there like an idiot and tell me that you beat the stuffing out of him. Hellooooo, are you listening to me?"

Dominic Andretti fell in love on the spot. Not only was this the most gorgeous woman he had ever seen, but she had a mouth on her. Any girl he brought home to his boisterous Italian family would have to be able to hold her own and this beauty wouldn't have any trouble doing that.

Ginger O'Dell, Tommy's mom, looked Dom over and demanded, "Hello, Mr. Policeman, are you deaf or just stupid?"

Dom dropped to his knee in front of Ginger, grabbed her hand and begged, "Will you marry me?"

Ginger laughed her head off and told Dom maybe they had better start with dinner and see where that led. Two months later they were engaged and three months after that they were married in an Irish/Italian wedding extravaganza. Ten months after that, Charlene, a.k.a. Charlie Andretti was born. The Andrettis moved out to Long Island to raise their family and probably would have stayed there their whole lives had they never taken that vacation to Oregon.

One day at work, Dom heard about a bunch of guys going on a trip to herd cattle. He could just see it, a bunch of New York City cops riding around on horseback trying to rope a bunch of unsuspecting cows. He had a good laugh at the image. Yet it got him to thinking about how much he always wanted to be a cowboy when he was growing up. When the guys asked him to come along, he declined, but he did stop by the AAA on his way home to pick up some cowboy-type vacation information for his family. When he told Ginger about his plan to take the girls to Oregon for a family get-a-way, she thought it was a great idea. Ginger grew up in New York City and loved nothing more than the idea of lots and lots of open land. So in June, when Charlie got out of school, they took the girls to the dude ranch in Scio. Three days later Dom bought the hardware store in Monteith. Ginger didn't even want to go back to Long Island to pack up the house. She just wanted to stay in the Willamette Valley forever. When they did get back to the Island, they sold their house and were ready to move in a record three weeks.

As soon as they got to Monteith, Ginger signed both of the girls up for square dancing, line dancing and horseback riding lessons. She was bound and determined to raise two little cowgirls. It turns out neither of them had any talent in those areas so she backed off and let them decide what kind of things they were interested in. Like their mother, both girls had a decided flare for fashion and makeup. They loved to play dress-up and teeter around the house in their mom's high heels. Ginger was delighted that her daughters were learning to express themselves through fashion. Although that wasn't always a common way of thinking in small towns, Ginger didn't care. She grew up in a big, dirty city and knew first-hand the kind of trouble kids could get into. So if her girls wanted blue hair or pink hair or purple hair, she was going to let them have it. Life was much easier when you had the confidence to be who you were.

Charlene

Willy would have done anything to have a big sister like Charlie. Not only was Charlie sixteen, with a driver's license, but she actually let Tommy go with her everywhere she went. If Charlie went to the pharmacy to look at new make-up, she would let Tommy tag along. If she went to the Hasty Freeze, Tommy got to go too. If Charlie was going to drive up and down First Street with her friends, where was Tommy, but in the back seat wedged between Beth Ellen and Jeannie. Willy had always wanted a big sister, but even in her wildest imaginings, she didn't think it would ever be as cool as it must be having Charlie for one. As soon as Mrs. Snodgrass talked to Mrs. Andretti and found out what a good driver Charlie was, Willy got invited to go with them whenever she wanted. Life in Monteith was getting better and better.

Her first week in Oregon, Willy found out that

Tommy's family were Presbyterians, just like her family. Willy told Tommy that she thought all Italians were Catholics. She found out the O'Dells had been practicing Presbyterians ever since they came to America from Ireland. So when Tommy's mom and dad got married, Mr. Andretti became a Presbyterian to keep marital harmony. No matter how it happened, Willy was delighted.

Willy spent her first Saturday night in Monteith sleeping over at the Andretti's house. She would meet up with her parents at church the next morning. When her parents saw her on Sunday they were more than a little shocked. The girls talked Charlie into washing and setting their hair so they would look gorgeous for church, as Jamie Armstrong, super-hunk of the seventh grade was also a Presbyterian. But that's another story. Charlie did Tommy's hair first. When she got to Willy's, she realized she had run out of the medium pink sponge rollers and the only ones left were the extra-small black ones. Willy told Charlie that her hair didn't curl very well any way, so it was probably better to use the small ones. After the thirty-two small rollers got wound into Willy's damp hair, she could hardly wait to see how fabulous she'd look the next morning. But when she woke up on Sunday, she only had twenty-eight rollers left in her hair. Once those twenty-eight rollers came out, she looked like she'd stuck her finger in an electrical outlet, with the exception of the four sections that came undone in the middle of the night. Those four sections were bone straight. The over-all effect was startling to say the least. Unfortunately, Willy didn't have time to rewash and dry her hair before church. So when Mrs. Andretti saw her, she dragged her daughter's new friend up to her bathroom to try to undo some of the damage. With a little mousse, a headband and loads of hair spray, Willy eventually wound up looking a tiny bit more normal. Of course she still didn't look anything like she had the last time her parents saw her.

Mrs. Snodgrass approached Charlie after church and asked how she liked being a big sister to another little girl. Charlie said having two little sisters was more fun than one. Mrs. Snodgrass assured Charlie that she was very appreciative of everything she was doing to make Willy feel at home. Then she asked Charlie to please never put Jello into Willy's hair. Because as much as she would like her daughter to be an individual some day, she would like for her to be her normal little girl just a little while longer. Charlie laughed and told her not to worry. She wouldn't do it even if Willy begged. Much relieved, Emma Jean Snodgrass joined her family in the church parking lot.

Charlene Rachael Andretti kept her word about never putting Jello into Willy's hair. If only Mrs. Snodgrass had thought to ask her to never cut her daughter's hair. Willy was bound to become an individual yet.

Georgianna Carbunkle

Georgianna Euphemia Bartlett was born on October the third, nineteen hundred and thirty-eight. She was born in a lovely house on Walnut Street in Monteith, Oregon that her father had bought for her mother as a wedding gift. The women in her family had lived in the Willamette Valley ever since Georgianna's great-grandparents moved there back in 1888. Georgianna had a wonderful childhood. Back in those days, electricity was just starting to show up in homes, indoor plumbing and telephones were rare in rural Oregon and the television hadn't even been invented. All and all, it didn't sound that great to Willy. But Mrs. C. assured her that it was ideal. Even though it was before her time, legend had it that in 1929, when the great depression started, the town really showed its true colors. Mrs. Carbunkle told the girls the whole town of Monteith helped each other out and when folks lost their jobs, they went to work in a community garden. That way everyone would have enough to eat. Those who didn't lose their jobs helped the gardeners buy shoes and coats and other necessities for their families. No one in the town had much, but what they had they shared and they got through those hard years just fine.

Georgianna had two brothers who were both younger than she was. Her brother Adam was only eleven months younger and her brother Johnny was four years younger. At that time, all the kids in Monteith went to school in a one-room schoolhouse right on the edge of town. They went there until the eighth grade. Then they started working alongside their parents. Georgianna's mother, Athena, was one of the few women in the Willamette Valley who had a job outside of the home. She ran a shop, known as The Willamette Wig Factory, with her mother, Aurelia and her Grandmother, Bella.

Bella, Georgianna's great grandmother, moved to Monteith in the Willamette Valley with her husband in 1888. She moved there from New York City where she had been the toast of the town. Bella's husband, Alfred, made his fortune in New York and announced one day that he was ready to see the Wild West. He convinced his wife to pack up their girls and move with him to Oregon. Bella always had an adventurous spirit and as much as she would miss

New York, she was ready to see what the West was like. Monteith, back in the 1880's, wasn't much of a town, but what was there was more breathtaking than you can imagine. Alfred hired half the men in town to build his family a home. A year later, they moved in and Bella declared that she was bored. She had help that did all the housework and gardening. More than anything, she wanted to bring a little of New York to her new town. Alfred asked her what she missed most about the city and after much thought, Bella declared she missed her hairdresser. Her hair hadn't been the same since they left and more importantly, the women in town looked worse than she did. Alfred asked her if she wanted to hire someone to come to Monteith to do her hair. But Bella decided it would be no fun to have gorgeous hair if the townswomen didn't as well. So after much thought, she decided to open a wig factory. That way, all the women of the Willamette Valley could have gorgeous hairdos, without taking time out of their busy lives to fix their hair themselves. Alfred thought she was crazy, but he loved his wife, and if that was going to make her happy, then so be it. He got the same men who built his house to get going on building his wife a wig factory right in the middle of town.

All of Monteith thought Bella was a bit eccentric,

too, but they liked her, so they didn't tell her. When the factory was built, Bella hired a wig craftsman from London to come and get her new business going. He taught several of the town folk how to make his wonderful wig creations and before they knew it, shops in New York City and Paris, were buying wigs from The Willamette Wig factory. No one saw it coming, but Bella brought a lot of jobs and prosperity to her new corner of the world.

The women in town still thought it was an unnecessary expense to own wigs for themselves so they refused to purchase them, even with the special discount Bella offered. That was when she decided to open an annex to her factory, which became kind of like the public library of wigs. For a one-time nominal fee, the women of the Willamette Valley purchased a wig ticket. They could use the ticket any time they wanted to come into The Annex and borrow a wig for a special occasion. All they had to do afterwards was wash and return it. The employees of the factory would restyle the wigs and return them to The Annex for future use. Bella didn't make any money on this side business, but she felt it her duty to keep the women of Monteith in good hair.

When she retired, Bella passed the shop on to her daughter Aurelia. When Aurelia retired, she passed the shop on to her daughter Athena, and Athena passed it on to her daughter, Georgianna. Georgianna had four boys and none of them stayed in town, so when she retired, she closed up shop. This was how once famous Willamette Wig Factory came into being and then was no more.

Monday

The first Monday in Monteith was a wash. Tommy and her family left for Long Island to visit her grandparents and would be gone for two weeks. Two weeks! What was Willy going to do now? Her mother suggested that she and Wendell ride their bikes to the town pool and look into getting summer swim passes. As much as Willy loved to swim, she felt very self-conscious about swimming in a pool full of strangers. But after spending the entire morning hanging around the house doing nothing, she decided she might as well just go and get her pass. After all, even if she didn't use it until Tommy came back, she would surely need it then.

Willy told Wendell to meet her in the garage in ten minutes and she would take him to the pool. Wendell did not understand they were just going for passes and showed up in his swim trunks, arm floaters and snorkel.

Willy rolled her eyes, "Wendell, we aren't staying at the pool to swim, we're just going to get our passes."

Confused, Wendell asked, "Why would we go and get them and not use them?"

Willy snapped, "Because I don't know anyone at the pool. You can go with me when Tommy gets back."

Wendell exclaimed, "No way Willy, I'm going swimming today and mom says you have to stay and watch me."

Well, this was just the icing on the cake, wasn't it? Willy stormed into the house and changed into the new hot pink bikini that she bought at The Glad Bag. She put her hair in a ponytail and then at the last minute decided to clip on her new fake belly button ring. Maybe it would give her courage. Heaven knew she could use a little of that.

Willy and Wendell rode their bikes the eight blocks to the public pool. They proceeded to the front desk where they would show their passes to get in and inquired about the summer fee. Willy filled in the amount on the check her mom sent with her and gave it to the high school kid working the desk. He told them their permanent passes would be mailed to them within a week and they should use their receipt to get in until that time. Willy instructed Wendell to go into the boy's locker room and take a shower. She would meet him in the pool area. She warned him not to actually go into the pool until she was there to watch him.

Willy went into the girl's locker room and discovered it was filled with girls around her age. She thought she was going to be sick. Why did she care so much what they thought, anyway? She already had a new best friend so she didn't really need them. This is what she told herself to give her the courage to take her shower and make it out to the pool without getting sick.

When she got there, Wendell was already waiting on the deck where all the kids left their towels while they swam and where they laid out in between dips in the pool. He put his towel right next to a group of kids about Willy's age. With a deep breath for courage, Willy joined her brother.

Wendell saw his sister and announced, "Hey, Will, I'm gonna take off now, okay?"

"Okay, but stay in the shallow end right next to the life guard chair and if I'm not here when you get back, I just went for a soda or something, so don't leave."

"Yeah, whatever." he answered as he ran toward a group of boys in the pool.

Willy lay her towel down and put on sunscreen, all

the while trying to decide what to do next. She decided to lie down on her stomach and listen to the kids talking next to her. Maybe she could get an idea of what grade they were in. One girl was talking about how excited she was about cheerleader tryouts. She was going to practice all summer. Her friend told her that she was a shoo-in to captain the seventh-grade squad and that she shouldn't worry about it. The seventh-grade squad? Willy covertly looked over to check the two girls out. They were clearly part of the popular group if one of them was going to captain the seventh-grade cheerleading squad.

Sure enough, they were cute in that perfect "cheerleader" way, totally tiny and blonde. Yuck! Were cheerleaders the same everywhere you went? Willy discovered their names were Tiffany and Bree. Their names were the same too, she decided. She was so engrossed in what the two girls were saying that she didn't notice the boy who walked over to her and stood right by her towel.

"Your hair looks much better today."

Willy looked up and was astonished to see the cutest boy ever. "Excuse me, what?"

Tiffany and Bree stopped talking and just stared at Willy. They hadn't noticed her before. But at that moment, they wondered who the redhead was and why on earth Jamie Armstrong was talking to her.

"I said your hair looks much better today than it did at church yesterday."

At church? Willy never saw this gorgeous boy at church. Surely she would have noticed him if he was there. Yet he must have been there if he saw her hair. Her hair… oh man, this was humiliating. He had seen her hair!

Willy stammered, "Uh, thank you, I guess. I was just trying something new. Guess it didn't work out too well."

"Oh," answered Jamie, "it was fine. This is just much better."

Jamie gave her another blinding smile as he strode off toward his own towel. Willy just watched him walk by with her mouth open when she heard one of the girls next to her ask, "Who is that girl and why was Jamie Armstrong talking to her?"

One of the cheerleaders had a bee in her bonnet over Jamie talking to her. Willy didn't know what to do. She could either turn to them and introduce herself or pretend that she hadn't heard them. They were clearly irritated by her very existence so she pretended she didn't hear them. Willy wasn't exactly popular in Mason, but she had gone to school there her whole life so at least she knew everyone. She had friends who were cheerleaders, friends who were into sports and still other friends who were in the band. She, herself, played the clarinet, ran track and was seriously considering trying out for the junior high cheerleading squad when she found out that her family was moving. But now, before she hardly knew a soul, she was about to become disliked by two of the popular girls in her new class. That was not a good sign.

Willy decided to get up and get a soda. That might clear her head and keep her from having to listen to the cheerleaders talk about her. Maybe if she pretended she hadn't heard them, she'd actually have a chance to be friends with them some day. She got up, grabbed her coin purse and just as she walked by, Tiffany or Bree stuck a foot out and tripped her. Willy stumbled for about five feet, before falling smack down on the cement, right on her knees. It hurt like crazy and all she wanted to do was cry. Before she could get up on her own, Jamie Armstong ran over and helped her to her feet.

Jamie looked at the cheerleaders and blasted, "Nice going, Tiff! What's wrong with you anyway?"

Tiffany was clearly alarmed that Jamie was yelling at her and replied, "I have no idea what you're talking about. I was just stretching my leg."

Jamie turned his back on them and said to Willy, "Here, let me get your stuff for you and I'll help you to the first-aid station."

So off went Willy with the cutest boy she had ever seen. Normally, this would be a good thing, even with the blood running down her legs. But she knew all too well she had just made two sworn enemies and that is no way to start life in a new town. Boy did she hate Mondays.

Potluck

There was going to be a potluck at church next Sunday right after services. Willy didn't want to go because Tommy wasn't going to be there, but she did want to see Jamie again. He had gotten her to the first-aid station last Monday but just before they walked in, one of his friends interrupted by splashing him from the pool. So instead of going in with her, Jamie smiled his dazzling smile and told her he'd see her in church on Sunday. Then he dove in the water to get even with his friend. Willy couldn't think of a better reason to go to church or a better reason not to curl her hair than seeing Jamie Armstrong again.

Willy changed dresses four times before deciding on her butter yellow sundress with the white sandals. She brushed her hair about a million times to get it super shiny then put it up in a pony-tail, remembering that Jamie complimented her on that style. Just as she was walking out to the car, she had a horrible thought. What if Tiffany and Bree were Presbyterians too? She would just die! They couldn't be, could they? After all she didn't see them at church last Sunday, but then again, she didn't remember seeing Jamie there either. She could hardly breathe the whole way there. It wasn't until her family sat down in a pew that she started to feel better. The church was full and she didn't see either one of the cheerleaders. She did see Jamie though and he gave her a little wave. Willy took a moment to say a prayer of thanks for her good fortune.

After the service ended, the Snodgrass family congregated in the fellowship hall with the rest of the parishioners for the potluck. Willy's mom and dad talked to a lot of different people and of course Wendell was off rough-housing with a bunch of boys. It was starting to feel a little more like home here in Monteith. Jamie Armstrong approached Willy and apologized, "I'm sorry I didn't get a chance to introduce myself at the pool Monday. My name is Jamie."

Willy was sure that her face turned as red as her hair, "Thank you for helping me to the first-aid station. My name is Willy."

"Willy, huh? What's that stand for?"

Willy cringed, "It stands for Wilhelmina."

"Wow, that's a pretty exotic name! I like it. What

grade are you going to be in?"

Willy answered, "I'm going into the seventh grade. How about you?"

Willy already knew that Jamie was going to be in the seventh grade, too. Tommy had told her that last week, but she didn't want him to think she had already been talking about him.

Jamie proclaimed, "Hey, that's great. Me too! So will Tiffany and Bree, the girls from the pool. Don't worry about them, though. Tiffany is just mad that I broke up with her before school let out last year."

Now Willy knew why Tiffany tripped her. "You went out with her last year?"

He replied, "Yeah, for about a month, but to tell the truth, she's just not my type. She's a little mean." Then he laughed, "I'm sure you probably figured that one out on your own, huh?"

Willy grimaced, "You could say I have the scabs to prove it."

Jamie introduced Willy to a couple of other kids that would be in the seventh grade in the fall. By the time the potluck was over, Willy thought the move to Oregon might have been the best thing that ever happened to her. Thank you, Jamie Armstong!

Wig Factory

It had been a whole ten days since Tommy left to visit her grandparents in New York and Willy began to think she might die of boredom. For obvious reasons, she had been avoiding the swimming pool since that first day. She wanted to wait until Tommy got back so she could get the lowdown on Tiffany and Bree. Her mother's aunt Jezabelle used to always tell her, "Don't court trouble." She realized this sage advice definitely applied to her current situation. Wendell had been going to the pool with his new friends from down the street, so he wasn't complaining to their mom that Willy wouldn't take him. Mrs. Snodgrass was busy making friends with the ladies from the Welcome Wagon, and Mr. Snodgrass was hard at work in his new job. No one seemed to notice Willy hanging around the house all day with nothing to do.

Willy woke up feeling like she'd go crazy if she

didn't get out for a little while. So she decided she'd ride her bike around town and try to get a feel for where everything was. She got up, ate breakfast, put on shorts and a tank top and then headed for her ten-speed in the garage. Willy figured she'd start out slowly and ride up and down Carousel Lane. Once she had done that about twenty times, she ventured towards First Street. Since she had already been down First Street with Tommy, she kind of knew where she was going. She took the same path she and Tommy had taken the week before. After covering the main road, she rode up Church Street, then over to Walnut and before she realized it, she was turning down the alleyway leading to the abandoned wig factory.

The alley that led to the factory was a little spooky. The first thing Willy noticed was that it was about ten degrees cooler there because both sides of the alley were lined with huge oak trees. The trees formed a canopy over the tops of people's garages and effectively blocked the sun. It was enchanting, really. But something was very different. Willy started to get tingles up and down her arms. For a second, it felt like she was slipping back in time. She convinced herself that she was being ridiculous. But then, out of the corner of her eye, she thought she saw a woman in a long black dress with a bustle at the back, walk around the corner. Who was that? Willy thought she had better just turn around and go home. But there was nothing to do at home and no one there. She decided to hang out for a minute and see if any other strange stuff happened. Willy got off her bike, propped it up against the side of someone's garage and waited.

That's when she noticed a crowd of people surrounding an amazing carousel. The merry-go-round was about fifty yards behind the factory and it was playing old-fashioned music. The people on it were dressed up in old-fashioned costumes too. "This is insane." Willy thought. She must be hallucinating. She'd never heard of a carousel in Monteith before. So instead of walking toward the factory she decided to check out the crowd to see if it was real or a mirage. There's no way it could be real. Yet the closer she got, the stronger the image became. Children ran around squealing excitedly, dogs barked, people were nibbling on bags of popcorn. It felt like a veritable carnival.

Willy stopped and stared at the most astounding scene. The carousel was huge and it was filled with creatures she had never seen on a merry-go-round. There was a huge fish, a frog, a rooster, a griffin, a dragon… the list just went on and on. There were only a handful of horses, which is the standard animal for this ride. Amazing!

Willy was about to get in line in case the illusion was real, when a sweet little dog ran up to her and started barking. Willy bent down on her knees and let him sniff her fingers. Then she scratched the back of his neck. While she was playing with him, she heard someone call out, "Jingle Bennet, where have you gone off to? Jingle!" Willy looked up and saw a girl about her age walking straight towards her. The girl was dressed up like everyone else in her vision. She had on a long, light blue dress with short, puffed sleeves and a lace collar. She also had on white gloves and was carrying a matching parasol. Her hair was blonde and curly and was pulled back from her face and tied with a lace bow.

The girl announced, "There you are Jingle. Why do you always run off after your bath? I swear you're giving mother fits." She warned, "If you don't start behaving soon, she's liable to boot you out once and for all."

Willy just stood there and stared at the girl and wondered why she seemed familiar to her. It was then that the mystery girl finally noticed Willy. "Hello. I'm Aurelia Bennet. You're Wilhelmina, right?"

Willy was positively transfixed. "Yes, yes I am." Then giving herself a mental shake asked, "You can see me? You know who I am?"

Aurelia laughed, "Of course I can see you, silly. Why wouldn't I be able to see you?"

Willy wondered, "Where am I?"

Aurelia smiled, "You're in the town of Monteith in the Willamette Valley in Oregon."

"No I'm not. That's where I was when I went on my bike ride, but now, I have no idea where I am."

Aurelia grabbed Willy's hand and gave it a bit of a squeeze and then she smiled. "This is kind of hard to explain, so try to keep an open mind, alright?"

Willy gave her a feeble smile, "Okay."

Aurelia explained, "From what I understand from my mother, you met my granddaughter Georgianna Bartlett a few days ago."

Willy gasped, "Your granddaughter? Are you kidding? What are you talking about? You're like, twelve. How can *you* have a granddaughter?"

"Oh, dear, I told you this wasn't going to be easy for you to understand. Now, just take a deep breath and listen. "My name is Aurelia Bennet, my mom's name is Bella Bennet, and my granddaughter's name is Georgianna Bartlett. But you know her as Georgianna Carbunkle. Do you remember meeting Georgianna last week?"

"Georgianna? Do you mean Mrs. Carbunkle, the little old lady on Walnut Street?"

Aurelia nodded and smiled, "Yes, I do. That's our Georgie. She's such a sweetheart."

Astonished, Willy asked, "The little old lady who gave me cookies is your granddaughter? What's going on here, are you a ghost or something?" When she saw the look on Aurelia's face she added, "Oh wow, I think I'm gonna throw up."

"You're not going to throw up. Pull yourself together and listen to me. Do you remember Georgie telling you about the wig factory?"

Willy nodded, "Yes, I remember. But what does any of this have to do with the wig factory?"

Aurelia answered, "I'll tell you. My mother opened up the factory four years ago, when my family moved here from New York. I started working at The Annex last month when I turned twelve. My daughter Athena started working with us when she turned twelve, and Athena's daughter, Georgie, did the same thing. Are you following me?"

Willy shook her head, "Not in the least." Then she demanded, "Are you all twelve? Are you all in the shop now? Are you or are you not a ghost?"

Aurelia smiled calmly, "Wilhelmina, I am going to answer all of your questions but it is going to take a little patience on your part, alright?"

"Fine, but just tell me, are you a ghost?"

"We are not fond of the word ghost. Mother and

I, and my daughter Athena, are more like angels. But we are angels on a mission and that's where you come in."

Willy announced, "Angels on a mission. That sounds like an old 'Charlie's Angels' movie."

Aurelia smiled, "I think they came a little after my time."

"Aurelia, what exactly *is* your mission?"

She answered, "Our mission is to get little Georgie to reopen the wig factory again. Why she closed it, I'll never know, but what I do know is that the factory needs to open again, and soon."

Willy asked, "Why do you think I'm the one to make that happen?"

"Well, Willy, Georgie was supposed to have three sons and a daughter, but there was a little mix-up and she wound up with four sons. Do you remember her telling you what she was going to name her daughter?" Willy nodded, so Aurelia continued, "She was going to name her daughter Wilhelmina. You see, the women in our family have always had at least one daughter to take over the factory and poor Georgie just had boys. We think she closed the factory when Athena died because she didn't want to work there alone. It made her sad that she didn't have a daughter of her own. That's where you come in."

"What do you mean, that's where I come in? I may be named Wilhelmina, but I'm not a member of your family."

Aurelia replied, "That's where you're wrong. You may not be Georgie's daughter, but you *are* a member of our family. Unfortunately, that's a story for another time. I think you should leave now and think about everything I've said. When you're ready, come back and I'll tell you more."

With those parting words, Aurelia Bennet stood up, picked up Jingle and walked down the street. Willy shook her head trying to make sense out of what just happened when she realized that she was standing in the middle of the alley all alone. Aurelia was gone, Jingle was gone and the crowd of people around the carousel was gone. As Willy moved toward the area where the phantom crowd disappeared, she discovered one very interesting thing. There really was a carousel in town. But the carousel existing in her time was in ruins.

Family History

Willy rode her bike home in a daze. As much as she thought she might be losing her mind, she also knew that what just happened was no dream. She couldn't understand why, but Willy knew she'd actually met Aurelia Bennet. Among the many things she couldn't figure out was why did Aurelia think that she, Wilhelmina Snodgrass, was part of her family? Willy knew her mom's maiden name was Fischer and her dad's mom's maiden name was Sinclair. Not a Bennet, Bartlett or Carbunkle among them. She'd have to ask her parents about it.

Three hours later, Willy was still home alone with no sign of anyone in her family. Had they totally forgotten about her? Willy went to the family room and started pulling old photo albums off the shelf. She was looking for someone with the first name of Bella, Aurelia, Athena, Georgianna, or someone with the last name of Bennet, Bartlett or Carbunkle. She was going to figure out how she was related to Mrs. C. and the strange girl in the alley. She found her grandmother Wilhelmina's wedding photo. Her gram had married Willy's grandfather, Jerome Snodgrass. But that was the oldest photo she could find in the family albums. She wondered where she could find more family history. That's when it hit her. She might learn more in her grandmother's bible! Willy knew the bible had been in her family since the mid-eighteen-fifties. So if this family connection was on the Snodgrass side of the family, she was bound to find some clue. Willy pulled the bible off the book shelf and carried it over to the dining room table. The first page had a listing of all the marriages and births on her dad's side.

Benjamin Barnes married Charmaine Le Fleur
August 16, 1858
Bella Barnes - October 7,1860
Jerome Barnes - November 12, 1862

This particular bible must have passed down to Jerome on his wedding, because the next entries read:

Jerome Barnes married Charlotte Gibbs
July 4, 1897
Chantelle Barnes - June 20, 1899
Loraine Barnes - Dec. 13, 1900
Adelia Barnes - Feb. 03, 1902

Adelia must have received the bible, because the next entry was:

Adelia Barnes married James Sinclair
September 30, 1925
Chere' Sinclair - October 3, 1926
John Sinclair - April 17, 1928

Willy was seeing a pattern here. The bible was passed down to the youngest child of the family. This meant Wendell was going to get the family bible. That wasn't going to happen if she had anything to say about it!

John Sinclair married Adele Simms
June 26, 1952
Wilhemina Sinclair - March 16, 1957

Wilhelmina Sinclair married Jeromy Snodgrass
January 12, 1967
Gillian Elaine Snodgrass - February 6, 1978

John Adam Snodgrass - September 25, 1980

The last entry was of her parents' marriage and hers and Wendell's births. Willy read through the names again and again and the only one that caught her eye was Bella Barnes. Wasn't Bella the name of the lady who started the factory? If Bella had married someone with the last name of Bennet, then she would be her great, great, great, great aunt, as well as Mrs. C.'s grandmother. As soon as she screwed up her nerve to go back to the wig factory, she was going to find out.

Company

Willy thought about going back to the alley every day since she'd discovered it. It wasn't that she lacked the courage, exactly. She just didn't want to have this adventure all by herself. So she decided she would wait for Tommy to come home and then casually suggest they go and explore the wig factory together. Willy had no intention of telling her friend about meeting Aurelia. She would just wait and see if her ghostly ancestor made contact with her while Tommy was around. That was the reason Willy waited four whole days to go back to the alley.

Tommy called Willy as soon as she walked in the door from her trip to let her friend know she was home. The girls talked for half-an-hour about Tommy's vacation. Tommy had a great time in New York. She saw both her mom and her dad's families. She even got to call the numbers at her grandma Andretti's bingo night at the Nyack Home for seniors. Her grandma won thirty-eight dollars and split it with Tommy, telling her she was her good luck charm. Tommy didn't spend a penny of the money on her trip because she wanted to use it to take Willy out to lunch at The Plucky Pig when she got back home. The Plucky Pig was a diner on First Street and even though the name was horrendous, the food was out of this world.

Willy and Tommy made plans to meet at the Snodgrass's house at eight-thirty the following morning. They intended to ride their bikes around town, have lunch and maybe go to the swimming pool later in the afternoon. Tommy was so excited to see her new friend she showed up fifteen minutes early. Willy was already waiting for her. After a quick hug hello, the girls took off toward First Street. On the way there, Willy said, "You know, Tommy, I've been thinking about that wig factory ever since Mrs. Carbunkle told us about it. You wanna go check it out?"

Tommy exclaimed, "You bet I do! I can't believe I never knew what that place was. It's kind of cool isn't it? I mean an old wig factory right here in Monteith? I would have never imagined."

The girls rode towards Walnut Street and turned left into the alley. Willy started to get seriously nervous. When they entered the alley, everything seemed perfectly normal. Willy looked for Jingle and Aurelia, but she didn't see anything out of the ordinary.

"Hey, Willy," Tommy shouted, "Let's prop our bikes over here by this wall and explore on foot."

Pointing behind them, Willy asked, "Tommy, did you know about the old carousel behind the factory building?"

Tommy nodded, "Sure, but there's nothing to see now. It's all in ruins. I hear the town council is going to tear it down."

Willy gasped, "No! Why would they do that? It's so beautiful!"

Tommy laughed, "Beautiful? It's a wreck! It's also kind of dangerous because it's falling apart."

Willy realized the carousel looked nothing like it did in its heyday. She also noticed a fence had been constructed around it to keep people out. "Why doesn't the town council rebuild it? I mean, how cool would that be?"

Tommy shrugged, "It would be cool but it would probably cost a fortune."

Forgetting the carousel for the time being, the girls got off their bikes and headed toward the factory. The building definitely looked like it had been built over a hundred years ago. It was a three-story brick structure with ivy growing all over it.

Willy saw some writing under the ivy and began to pull some of it off so she could see what it said. As Willy pulled, the ivy seemed to pull right back at her. This was ridiculous. Why wasn't the ivy coming off? Yet the harder Willy pulled, the harder it pulled back at her. Willy was about to give up when the vine started to move all by itself. It arranged itself in such a way that it formed an arrow, an arrow pointing around the building towards the fire escape. Willy decided to follow it and called for Tommy to join her.

"Tommy, come here. Let's see what's around the corner."

Both girls walked around the side of the building where they noticed a fire escape that started at the second floor and went up to the roof.

Willy asked, "Why would the ladder start on the second floor?"

Tommy explained, "If there's a fire, you jump out the window onto the fire escape. You see the ladder by the landing? You just unhook a latch and the ladder falls to the ground. That's so no one from the ground can climb up and break into the building. That's how a lot of them work in New York."

Willy was impressed by her friend's knowledge. Being that the girls couldn't get to the ladder to climb up the fire escape, they decided to look through the windows on the first floor. They could hardly see anything through the grime-covered glass, but Willy did glimpse a little white dog. Was that Jingle? Willy called Tommy over. This was her chance to find out if she was stark raving crazy.

"Tommy, come here. Look into this window and tell me what you see."

Tommy went over, peeked in and declared she couldn't see much because the windows were filthy.

Willy insisted, "Just keep looking. Are you sure you don't see anything?"

"Well, I think I see a very old-fashioned sofa. Oh my gosh, is that a dog sitting on the couch? What is a dog doing in there? Willy, we have to rescue him."

Willy peeked in the window again and saw Jingle sitting on the couch wagging his tail. Jingle barked a greeting.

"Hey Jingle, is that you boy?"

Jingle jumped down off the couch and ran to the window, enthusiastically wagging his tail.

"Jingle?" Tommy asked, "How do you know the dog's name?"

Willy explained how she came down the alley the other day and met Jingle and his owner, Aurelia. What she didn't explain was that twelve-year-old Aurelia was Mrs. Carbunkle's grandmother. She wasn't ready to have Tommy think she was a total whack job, just yet. After all, just because Tommy could see Jingle, didn't mean she could see Aurelia.

"Willy, help me find a door or an open window or something. We have to help that poor dog get out."

The girls walked around the building and checked the doors and locks. They couldn't find a way inside. When they walked by the fire escape for the third time, they heard music playing. It seemed to be coming from inside the factory.

Alarmed, Tommy asked, "Willy, do you hear that?"

"Yep, I sure do. Sounds like music coming from the factory."

"This is totally wacky, but do you smell something?"

Willy replied, "If you mean oatmeal cookies, then yeah, I do. Doesn't it kind of smell like it's coming from the factory?"

Just as the two girls were considering running down the alley to their bikes, the ladder on the fire escape slid down to the ground right in front of them. They both nearly jumped out of their skin in shock. Tommy actually stumbled backwards and fell right on her butt.

"Willy, I can't be sure, but I think I might have wet my pants."

Willy smiled, "I know it's a little scary, but I think

I know who made the ladder slide down. I think its Aurelia, you know, Jingle's owner?" Willy still didn't tell Tommy that Aurelia was a ghost or an angel on a mission or whatever she called herself. Instead she held out her hand and said, "Come on Tommy, let's climb up."

Willy headed for the stairs and Tommy was right on her heals. Tommy asked, "Do you think we should? I mean isn't it trespassing or something?"

"I think we were invited in, Tommy. When you're invited it's not trespassing."

Cautiously the two girls finally climbed up the fire escape. They stopped at the first landing and peeked through the second-floor window. All they saw was old factory equipment. Then, even more nervously, they continued up to the third floor. They stopped on the landing to catch their breath and that's when they heard the music. Clinging together, they looked through the window. What they saw nearly caused them both to fall over. The room they were looking at was a very lovely Victorian parlor. There were three people in the room; a beautiful lady about her mom's age and two girls about her and Tommy's age.

Aurelia looked out the window and saw the girls. With a big smile on her face she greeted, "Willy, Tommy, come in! We've been expecting you."

Great, Willy thought. They were expected by ghosts. The Willamette Valley was proving not to be a normal place.

Introductions

The pretty lady in the parlor was named Bella. She invited Willy and Tommy to sit down and asked them if they would like some cookies. The girls helped themselves and as soon as everyone was settled, Bella started to talk. She introduced herself and then asked Willy if she had figured out how they were related. Willy asked if Bella had married a man with the last name of Bennet. Bella answered in the affirmative. Willy went on to tell Bella that she, Wilhelmina Rhonda Snodgrass, must be her great, great, great, great niece then.

Tommy looked at her friend like she was a complete fruit loop. "Uh, Willy, call me crazy, but I'm pretty sure your great, great, great, great aunt would be dead by now."

The four other occupants of the room smiled at Tommy as she made this proclamation. That's when Tommy started to clue in. "Holy freakin' cow, are you a ghost? What am I even saying? Ghosts don't exist. This is crazy!"

Everyone stared at Tommy as she carried on. They continued to quietly smile at her. Tommy finally sat down and took a bite of her cookie, all the while refusing to make eye contact with the other people in the room. She took a deep breath and concluded, "You're all ghosts, right? With the exception of Willy, that is." When Bella nodded her head, Tommy declared, "Oh, well, there it is then. I'm ready for the nut house. Funny farm, here I come! I hope the loony bin has an opening!"

Bella grinned as Tommy continued talking to herself, "Tommy dear, are you quite finished? That was a lovely dramatic presentation, but we have work to do. Are you going to be a productive member of this meeting or should you go?"

Tommy gasped, "Go? I'm not going anywhere. This is the coolest thing that's ever happened to me!"

Bella asked, "Cooler than blue hair, Tommy?"

"Much. You know about the blue hair, huh?"

"Oh my, yes. We've had our eye on you. We've been trying for six months to get Wilhelmina's dad that promotion at work. If it didn't happen when it did, we were going to ask you to help us, Tommy. However, we would have had to revise the plan some, given that your hair is always so odd."

Tommy was confused, "Why wouldn't you have asked me first?"

Bella explained, "We would be truly delighted for your assistance Tommy, but Wilhelmina was simply our first choice as she is a blood relative. However, with the two of you working together, I'm sure we'll have this factory reopened in no time."

Willy said, "Aunt Bella, Aurelia never did say why the factory needed to be reopened."

Bella explained to the girls that they would have that information when it was needed. But right now, they had bigger fish to fry, as the saying goes. Bella introduced Aurelia to Tommy. Then she introduced the other twelve year old girl, who was Aurelia's daughter, Athena.

Tommy asked, "How exactly is it that Aurelia and Athena are both twelve? And Bella, you hardly look old enough to have died."

Bella explained, "You see, the age I appear to you now, is the age I was when I opened The Willamette Wig Factory. The age you see both Aurelia and Athena is the age *they* were when they started working here. We all have such fond memories of our first days at the factory. So, even though we all lived to be rather old ladies, we like to look like we did in the old days. Understand?"

"Not really," Tommy answered. "But there's so much I don't understand that I'm not even going to try."

Bella commented that sometimes in life, you just had to accept things and agreed perhaps this was one of those times. She continued to tell the girls about the plan she orchestrated to get Georgianna to reopen the family business. It was a plan involving a little bit of sacrifice on Willy's part. It was a plan involving scissors.

The Plan

Willy did not like Bella's plan at all. The problem was that the move to Oregon was her fault. These ghostly relatives of hers were responsible for her dad's promotion and the only reason he got promoted was because of their plan. So it would be pretty low of her to refuse to go along with it. It wasn't going to be easy though and was surely going to cause her some trouble at home. But Bella swore the girls to secrecy. They were not allowed to tell anyone, including their parents about their plan, the factory or Willy's new found relative, Georgianna Carbunkle, until further notice.

The plan is why Tommy and Willy wound up in the Andretti's bathroom begging Charlie to cut their hair. Charlie had no problem cutting Tommy's hair. She was used to doing odd things to her little sister's head. She just didn't want to cut Willy's hair because she was afraid Mrs. Snodgrass would be upset. Willy assured her that her mom wouldn't mind at all and if Charlie didn't agree to cut her hair, she was going to do it herself and then it would be awful for sure. Charlie continued to resist. She offered to give Willy the money to have it professionally cut at The Hair Hutch, but Willy wouldn't take it. She said she needed her hair cut that very day and didn't have time to make an appointment with Sheila McNut. This went on and on for about thirty minutes before Charlie finally caved in. After all, she had promised Mrs. Snodgrass she wouldn't dye Willy's hair blue, not that she wouldn't cut it.

Charlie did Tommy's hair first. She gave her little sister a blunt cut to the shoulders, and then she dyed the bottom inch jet black. By the time Tommy came back from New York, her hair was blonde and very normal looking again, so she was very ready for this new look. Once Tommy's change was complete, it was Willy's turn. Charlie asked her what kind of style she wanted. Willy paused, then took a great big deep breath and finally declared she wanted a short cut, something showing off her ears. Willy had never in her life worn her hair short and she never wanted to, but there was something bigger at work here and she knew she had to go for it.

Charlie was totally shocked that Willy wanted such a drastic change. Her sister's new friend just didn't seem the type. When she expressed her concerns out loud, Willy proclaimed, "Oh, I'm the type all right. I've been ready for this for ages." Through gritted teeth, she tried to sound excited, "Let's do this already!"

Willy closed her eyes and Charlie started cutting. It took her about twenty-five minutes of snipping and trimming, trimming and snipping, before it was done. Charlie looked a little uncertain at the final outcome, but it *was* short and it did show off Willy's ears. Willy looked in the mirror in absolute horror. This was it. The plan had just been set in motion.

Willy thanked Charlie, hoping she sounded sincere, which she didn't. Then Tommy grabbed her traumatized friend by the hand and dragged her out of the bathroom. "Come on, let's go. We've got to get to Mrs. C.'s."

The girls got on their bikes and took off down Carousel Lane. On the way to Mrs. Carbunkle's, Willy wondered what Jamie Armstrong was going to think about *this* hairstyle. In the excitement of the wig factory, Willy hadn't even told Tommy she'd met Jamie. She hadn't told her about Tiffany or Bree either. Oh boy, this summer was just getting more and more complicated.

It was a little after noon when the girls arrived at Mrs. Carbunkle's door. They rang/chirped the bell and once again heard, "Hold your horses. I'll be there when I get there!"

That made them both smile. Mrs. C. certainly was a character. When their old friend opened the door she looked the girls over and declared, "Tommy, your hair is so you. I'm inclined to like this style quite a bit more than some of the others you've sported."

Then she looked at Willy with such pity Willy didn't even have to act when she burst into tears. "Oh, my dear Wilhelmina, your hair is quite atrocious, isn't it? What ever were you thinking?" She scurried the girls inside and announced, "Let's see if some sugar cookies can lend a little perspective to this catastrophe."

Willy and Tommy followed Mrs. C. into the kitchen and sat down at the table. They each ate two cookies in complete silence. Then Mrs. C. finally spoke. "Wilhelmina, do you want your hair to look this way?" Willy shook her head dejectedly.

"Well, then there's no hope for it. We're going to have to take a trip over to the wig factory and see if we can find something for you to wear until that unfortunate style grows out a little." She shook her head, "I haven't been inside that building in over thirty years. You're going to have to give me a moment to remember where I put my keys."

Tommy gave Willy a covert smile. The first stage

of the plan was under way. Mrs. C. was going to unlock the door to the factory!

Ten minutes after she started looking for the keys, Mrs. C. called out to the girls to shake their tail feathers. She was ready to go. The friends left their bikes at the house and walked to the factory, one on either side of Mrs. Carbunkle.

Tommy broke the silence first, "Mrs. C., why did you close the factory? I mean it's not like the women of Oregon stopped caring about their hair, right?"

"Thomasina, dear, the fine ladies of Oregon have always cared about their hair. I closed the shop because it was very lonely going in there all alone. When my mother died I just lost the heart for it, that's all." Looking sad, she confessed "It's going to be very difficult to walk through those doors again, because everywhere I look, there are going to be memories; wonderful memories of times long gone."

Mrs. Carbunkle seemed very distressed as she walked slowly towards their destination. She grabbed each of the girls' hands and gave them a squeeze. "If it wasn't for poor Wilhelmina's unfortunate haircut, I don't think I could have found the gumption to go back. But desperate times call for desperate measures. That's what my grandmother Aurelia used to say."

Willy didn't say what she was thinking, but she was thinking, "That's what Aurelia *still* says!"

Into The Rabbit Hole

Willy, Tommy and Mrs. C. finally arrived at their destination. It felt like it took three hours to get there, probably because of the mixture of anxiety, nerves and expectation on the part of all three of them. Willy was mostly anxious, wondering what kind of wig they would find that would make her hair look less frightening. She hoped she wasn't jumping from the fat into the fire. Tommy was decidedly more nervous. She really did like the idea of three ghosts. It was just taking a bit of getting used to. She liked to think that just like the ghosts of The Willamette Wig Factory, she too would be fashion savvy, even in the afterlife. Mrs. Carbunkle was feeling a heavy dose of expectation. She expected to be flooded with memories the minute she set foot over the threshold. She expected to be very sad. She expected to feel very lonely. The reality was she was flooded with memories. She was a little sad, but she certainly wasn't lonely.

Mrs. Carbunkle led the girls down the old alleyway, right to the rather lovely front door of the factory. The girls didn't notice the front door when they were there earlier because it was totally covered by vines. But strangely, when Mrs. Carbunkle got her key out, the ivy moved of its own accord and uncovered a beautiful carved doorway. It was like the factory was welcoming back one of its own.

As soon as Georgianna Carbunkle unlocked the door, she stood there, frozen. Her hand shook and her eyes teared up ever so slightly. Tommy interrupted the moment by saying, "Come on Mrs. C., let's go in."

Georgianna took a deep breath and told the girls she never thought she'd set foot in the factory again. She vowed she would never go back alone. Willy reached out and took her friend's free hand and said, "But you're not alone. And even though you're not going in with your daughter, you could pretend. My name is Wilhelmina, after all."

That did it. Mrs. C. beamed, shook off her sad mood and declared she'd always planned to step through the doors with Wilhelmina and step through she would. There seemed to be an almost electric feel in the air. Somewhere deep down, when the trio entered the old abandoned factory, they knew all of their lives had changed in a very mysterious way. What they didn't know was that it wasn't just their lives, but the life of a very important person none of them dreamed they would ever meet, not in a million years!

What greeted the adventurers first was the abundance of dust. There was an immediate explosion of sneezes on the part of all three. Of course the dust was to be expected. No one, alive anyway, had set foot in the factory in many, many years. Mrs. C. declared that the first order of business was to open all of the windows and let out some of the filth. So before the girls could even take in the surroundings, they were scurrying around helping Mrs. C. air out the place. When they did stop to notice the room they were standing in, all they really saw were lots of sheets covering up the place. Mrs. C. instructed the girls to run around and pull the coverings off everything while she went back into the little kitchen to make them some tea. Willy and Tommy pulled and sneezed, sneezed and pulled until the whole room could be seen. It was positively breathtaking when it was revealed.

It looked like the décor was the same as it must have been when Bella opened the shop back in the 1880's. There were beautiful little settees stuffed with feathers. The ceiling had to be at least twenty feet high and there were two huge crystal chandeliers hanging from it. There was an enormous fireplace that had a stunning gold leaf oval mirror hanging above it. And on every surface possible were beautiful bronze statues of ladies.

When Mrs. Carbunkle walked back in with the tea service, she gave Willy and Tommy a brilliant smile and asked them if they liked what they saw. The girls talked over each other as they praised the room, wondering if the decorations were original. Where were the wigs? Why did it look more like a living room than a factory? Mrs. C. told them to sit down and pour the tea and she would tell them all about it. It turns out the décor was all Bella's vision. Every time Aurelia, Athena, or Georgianna brought something new into the factory to add their own stylistic touches, it would either get broken or disappear within minutes. It seemed a little fanciful, she told them, but the factory preferred to only wear the accessories in which Bella dressed it.

She explained the front room was the sitting room. This was where the ladies of Monteith gathered to discuss life, children, husbands, cleaning and as the years wore on, they came here to discuss jobs, war and the future of women. The Willamette Wig Factory was as much a social club and psychiatrist's office as it was a wig shop. Mrs.

Carbunkle declared like tradition decreed, they would sit down and enjoy a bit of tea and companionship before looking for the perfect wig to fix Wilhelmina's unfortunate situation.

The ladies sipped tea, chatted and took in the beauty of Bella's sitting room. They all felt like they were wrapped in loving arms. For a few moments no one said a word and Willy had the distinct impression like Alice, she had just fallen through the rabbit hole.

The Great Wig Search

After tea, Mrs. C. led the girls out of the room to begin the great wig search. It turned out that The Wig Annex was located down a grand hallway that led towards the back of the factory. The girls stepped into a room about twice as large as the front room. They immediately started pulling the sheets from everything even before Mrs. C. asked them to. When they were done, they were astonished by what they saw. There were old-fashioned display cases surrounding the perimeter of the room and every surface was covered with wooden wig-heads, all painted with faces and wearing different styles of hair. There must have been at least two hundred heads in the room, with styles that dated from 1889 to the most current styles when Georgianna closed the shop.

Willy wasn't even thinking of finding a wig for her everyday life. She was too busy imagining what she would look like in everything else. Then there was Tommy. Thomasina Franchesca Andretti, who liked nothing more than to change the color and style of her hair, actually started to cry. She just stood and stared as silent tears streamed down her cheeks. If Tommy were asked what her idea of heaven on earth was like, she would have described this room to a "T," right down to all the hair accessories arranged in the glass cases. She was home and she never wanted to leave.

The girls spent what seemed like hours trying on wigs and pretending they were ladies from the olden days. They preened and pranced and acted out skits for their own amusement. In the far corner of the room they even found a coat rack holding old-fashioned coats, so they put those on as well. Neither one of them noticed as Mrs. C. lovingly touched the displays, the walls and the draperies. Nor did they notice when she left the room and returned with a bucket of cleaning supplies and proceeded to clean the entire room. Mrs. C. moved around the ancient room like she was in her twenties, not eighties. But most interestingly, neither girl noticed Bella, Aurelia and Athena who were standing in a corner watching as The Annex came back to life.

As soon as Mrs. Carbunkle was finished cleaning, she told the girls that they had better get busy and find Willy a hairdo before it got so dark they couldn't see what they were doing. Tommy walked toward a light switch and asked, "Why don't we just turn a light on?"

Mrs. C. replied, "That is a lovely idea dear, but the electricity has been turned off for years and…"

Just as she was going to finish her sentence, Tommy flipped the switch and the huge chandelier hanging overhead flickered to life. Nobody moved or said a word. They were all transfixed by the glow the elegant fixture brought to the room. It was absolutely magical!

"How in the world did that happen?" Mrs. C. wondered. Then she added, "It didn't even occur to me that the gas stove used electricity when I made the tea. I should have known something was afoot then."

She made a note to herself to call the Willamette Valley Electric Company when she got home and ask what was going on. What she would find out would baffle her for days to come. Apparently, someone had called the Willamette Valley Electric the day before and had ordered all power restored to the old factory. Little did Mrs. C. know that Willy and Tommy already knew how the electricity came to be turned on. Bella, Aurelia and Athena had commenced with phase two of the plan.

Mrs. C. declared, "I'll have to sort this out with the electric company later, but right now, we must start looking for the perfect wig for dear Wilhelmina. Come girls, follow me. All the styles in this room are much too grown up and complicated for a girl of eleven-and-a-half. What we need to do, is go into the back and find a nice auburn wig that hasn't been cut and styled yet."

Mrs. C. led the girls into a back storeroom. Against the wall were three shelves that ran the whole length of the room. The shelves had boxes piled three deep on them. It kind of looked like the storage room in a shoe store, except inside the boxes was hair, not shoes. There were labels that read: short light blonde, long dark brown, light auburn, shoulder length…..the labels went on and on to cover every color, shade, and length imaginable. Tommy was in jeopardy of fainting dead away at all of the possibilities. She was going to do everything in her power to make sure this factory reopened for business.

Mrs. C. thoroughly checked out Wilhelmina's hair color before declaring it was definitely a medium auburn with honey highlights. She decided on a long length they would cut to fit Willy's needs. Then she led the girls into yet another room. This one was set up like an old-fashioned beauty salon. There were two gorgeous stuffed chairs, facing huge gilded mirrors. Willy hopped up into one and Tommy got into the other.

Mrs. C. put a smock over Willy's clothes and then proceeded to take the wig out of the box and place it on her young friend's head. They all laughed at the outcome because Willy looked more like a chia pet than a girl. Mrs. C. told the girls the wigs always came like that. That way there is never any question that there will be enough hair for any desired style. But in the case of Wilhelmina Snodgrass, they were definitely going to thin out the hair. Mrs. C. pulled a tray full of scissors out of the cabinet and started to work her magic. First, she thinned the hair way down. Then she started to trim some layers around her face, and before she could whistle Dixie, Willy looked better than she ever had in her entire life. These wigs were positively magic!

Rendezvous

Before leaving the wig factory, Willy and Tommy made a stop in the ladies' room. What with all the tea they drank and the bumpy bike ride ahead of them, they figured it was better to be safe than sorry. Mrs. C. pointed them in the direction of the bathroom and when they walked in, they found an elegantly appointed sitting area complete with a chaise lounge. They decided that must have been in case one of those ladies of old got hit with a case of the vapors and had to lie down. They had a good laugh over that image. But when they rounded the corner to the bathroom stalls they nearly wet their pants on the spot. Bella, Aurelia and Athena were staring right at them.

"Sweet mother of sheep! I'm gonna need to lay down on the chaise myself, but not before I tinkle. Everyone out of my way!" With that announcement, Tommy ran into a stall just in the nick of time.

Willy inquired, "Is there anyway you three could give us some kind of warning before scaring the beejeezus out of us? It's a good thing I have a wig now because I think my hair must have just turned stark white in fright."

Bella asked, "Willy dear, how else would you have preferred we make ourselves known to you? We don't want Georgie to see us and this has been our only real opportunity to get you alone."

After the initial scare and squabble had subsided, the girls were informed it was time to move on to the next phase of the plan. Since they didn't have time to talk then, Bella advised the girls to come back at ten-thirty the following morning, when they would be informed what would happen next.

Tommy and Willy walked Mrs. C. back to her house, thanked her for a wonderful afternoon, and then took off to grab a late lunch at The Plucky Pig, Tommy's treat.

Over cheeseburgers and chocolate shakes the friends relived their afternoon adventures. They discussed the factory, the amazing selection of wigs, how happy Mrs. Carbunkle was and last but not least, they speculated about their meeting tomorrow. They both wondered what Willy's ancestors had in store for them next.

When they were almost done with lunch, Willy

looked up to see that Bree and the hateful Tiffany had just walked into the restaurant. Willy remembered that she'd forgotten to tell Tommy about the incident at the pool. So she told her friend to take a look at who just walked into the diner. Willy asked her if she knew them.

Tommy responded, "There are only seventy-eight students in our entire class. Of course I know them. Why?"

Willy confessed the whole sordid affair of what happened at the swimming pool. She relayed that Tiffany was irritated that Jamie Armstrong stopped to talk to her. She explained how Tiffany tripped her and how Jamie took her to the first-aid station. Then she mentioned she spent the entire church potluck in Jamie's company.

Tommy took in all this information and commented. "Wow, you've been busy while I was gone! First of all, let me compliment your taste in friends. Jamie Armstrong is not only the most popular guy in our grade, he's also totally smart and really nice, so good job there. Unfortunately, your taste in enemies couldn't be worse. Tiffany Bowen and Bree Petersen are the sneakiest, most hateful, gossipy; nasty...should I go on or do you get my drift?"

Tommy told Willy the story about how Jamie and

Tiffany had been an item for a whole month the previous year. Apparently, Jamie had an older sister, Beth, who had Down syndrome. Beth was eighteen and very shy so she didn't come to town that often. One day, Tiffany unexpectedly stopped by the Armstrong's house to see Jamie and Beth answered the door. Tiffany acted horribly. She mumbled that she came to see Jamie, wouldn't make eye contact with Beth and then she just walked away. Jamie was watching the whole thing from a window upstairs. Normally, he would have run down and helped his sister out because he knew how much new people upset her, but he thought being that Tiffany was his girlfriend, they should probably meet.

Jamie was appalled by how Tiffany behaved. He couldn't understand how she could be so rude to his sister. The Armstrong family was not at all embarrassed that Beth had Down syndrome. They loved her to no end and thought she was the sweetest person in the world. That was the reason that Jamie knew he had to talk to Tiffany and find out why she acted like she did.

Jamie finally got Tiffany alone the next day at lunch. He mentioned that he'd heard she stopped by. Tiffany wanted to know who told him. He said his sister Beth told him. To which Tiffany asked, "You mean the retard?!"

"Tiffany, Beth has Down syndrome. We don't call her a retard."

Tiffany's hasty reply was, "But she is a retard, right? It must be so awful for you and your family."

She noticed Jamie's expression grow grim and tried to make things better by saying,

"I mean, jeez Jamie, you're so cute and popular. It must be really embarrassing for you."

That was when Jamie informed Tiffany that it wasn't embarrassing having Beth for a sister, but it was embarrassing having a snob for a girlfriend. He broke up with her then and there. Jamie heard from his friends that Tiffany went around school talking about Jamie's sister, "the retard." Tiffany thought by bad-mouthing Beth, people would be on her side in the breakup. It didn't work out that way. Jamie Armstrong had never said anything nasty about anyone else and people respected him for it. Tiffany, on the other hand, had nothing but mean things to say about almost everyone, so when it came to picking sides, Tiffany lost.

What made Tiffany even madder was that she really liked Jamie Armstrong. He was gorgeous, popular and talented. There was no one else in their grade she deemed worthy of dating her. That was why Tiffany vowed to get Jamie back and that was why she hated Wilhelmina Snodgrass.

Once Tommy filled her in on the whole story, Willy wanted to cry. How had she made such an archenemy so quickly? She had no idea what she was going to do and if she wasn't so pre-occupied with the goings on at the factory, she might seriously consider asking her parents to send her to boarding school. Just as she sucked out the last of her chocolate shake, she saw that Tiffany and Bree were walking their way. Tommy noticed too and said, "Brace yourself, here they come."

Before Tiffany or Bree got a chance to say anything, Tommy smiled brilliantly and declared, "Hey, you guys. How's your summer going? You both look positively gorgeous with those tans!"

Both Bree and Tiffany were a little surprised by Tommy's greeting. They thought for sure the red head would have told her all about the incident at the pool. For some reason, Bree and Tiffany both wanted to be friends with Tommy. Tommy figured it was because her mom used to be a famous model and that they wanted to be invited to Tommy's house to meet her. Little did they know that was NEVER going to happen.

Tiffany spoke up first. "Hey Tommy, I love your hair! Was that your mom's idea? She is so fashionable. I would be thrilled if she could help me out with my look someday."

Tommy exclaimed, "It *was* my mom's idea. Just look at what she did for my new friend, Willy. Isn't her hair amazing? My mom says redheads are more glamorous than anyone else."

Willy knew that Tommy was trying to help, but it seemed like she was making matters worse, much worse. Tiffany and Bree would eat her alive if they knew what her hair really looked like. Oh man, she wondered, would this never end?

Tiffany looked thoughtful, "I don't know, Tommy. I'm not going to say that your mom doesn't know what she's talking about. I just think redheads are kind of trashy. You know, totally common?"

Tommy got mad, "I'll tell my mom you said so. Now if you'll excuse us, we have to get going. There's a dreadful smell in here."

With that bold statement, Tommy dragged Willy to her feet and led her out of The Plucky Pig. Willy couldn't believe that Tommy had the guts to talk to Tiffany and Bree like that. She admired her for it but at the same time, she was having fantasies of giving her a sharp kick. After all, it was one thing to stand up for a friend. It was quite another to get her in worse trouble than she was in before.

Phase Two

Willy and Tommy were up and out of their respective houses by ten a.m. the next morning. They met at the bottom of Willy's driveway and were more than a bit excited to see what the day held in store for them. Willy told Tommy her parents thought her new hairstyle was fabulous and that Charlie was very talented. They got a good laugh over that. If they only knew the truth they would have been horrified. At ten-thirteen on the nose the friends parked their bikes next to the factory and decided to take a quick peek at the carousel before going in.

Willy asked, "What's the deal with the carousel, anyway? I mean why did the town let it fall into disrepair?"

Tommy replied, "I don't know why it wasn't kept up, but I do know that it was one of the premier menagerie carousels of the nineteenth century.

People came from all over the world to see it."

"What do you mean by menagerie?"

Her friend responded, "It means the carousel wasn't all horses like most. It had a wide variety of animals, some bizarre and some more normal." Pointing through the fence, she asked, "Did you see the dragon? That's my favorite. I can only imagine what the colors would look like if it weren't so faded."

Willy contemplated the ancient merry-go-round and replied, "I think I like the rooster best. I mean it's such a normal animal but so totally weird to find one on a ride like this."

Both girls noticed a shadow lurking on the carousel near the rabbit. Tommy called out, "Hey, you! What are you doing on that thing? It's not safe!"

A boy about their age turned to wave at them and then disappeared behind one of the animals

Willy gasped, "Who's the kid on the carousel?"

Tommy replied, "I have absolutely no idea." Shaking her head, she joked, "Probably another ghost." And with that she jumped and declared, "Speaking of ghosts, I think we have an appointment to keep."

Then the girls returned to the factory to keep their appointment. They forgot to ask Bella how they were supposed to get inside, but they figured they'd find a way.

When they walked up to the front door, they saw that as usual it was covered in ivy. They were just about to go around the corner to the fire escape when the ivy started to move and reveal the door. What was going on here? Tommy tried to open the door but it was locked.

She yelled, "What's the point of moving the ivy if you're not going to unlock the door?"

They were about to walk around the corner again when part of the vine pulled away from the building and grabbed Willy's arm. "What the heck? Owwww, you stupid vine, let me go!"

That's when she realized the vine was telling her to open the door. Willy put her hand on the knob and jiggled it a little to see if it was unlocked. She smiled at Tommy and then easily turned the handle. The door swung open all by itself.

"Nice. What, I'm not good enough to open your goofy door?" Tommy asked.

When the girls walked into the sitting room, they saw Bella, Aurelia and Athena were already assembled. The tea service was on the table and there was even a plate of cinnamon doughnuts. The girls eagerly joined them. When Tommy asked, "What's the deal with the door? How come Willy could open it and I couldn't?" She was clearly upset.

Athena took the opportunity to answer and told Tommy there was absolutely no offense meant. It was simply that Willy was family and the factory would only open willingly to a family member. She went on to explain that Tommy should be flattered though, because the door only opens to one of the family if they are alone or if they are with someone who has been accepted. Tommy had obviously been accepted. Tommy absorbed this information and although her feelings were still slightly bruised, it did make her feel a lot better.

It was Bella's turn to talk, "Alright, girls. We've been plotting all night trying to figure out the best way to commence with phase two. We've decided it's better to proceed slowly with Georgie than to push her too hard. Obviously, she has been strong enough to resist the pull of the factory for a number of decades. She has to think it's her idea to reopen it." With a note of doom, she added, "Otherwise, it may stay closed forever."

Willy asked, "So what exactly is it that you want us to do?"

"We've decided you should drop subtle hints to Georgie about how outdated and frumpy the women in the Willamette Valley look. Then tell her how much you love your wig and how many compliments you are getting on it. Things like that. Do you understand?" The girls assured Bella they understood fully and Tommy even started cooking up a sneaky plan of her own.

Tommy asked if they could have a tour of the factory and Bella thought that was a wonderful idea. The five of them proceeded up to the second floor where the factory part of the operation was located. Willy and Tommy weren't exactly sure what they were looking at, but were impressed none the less. There were industrial sewing machines to stitch the scull caps. Then there were stations set up where people would sit and hand knot the hair onto the caps. In the corner there were still bins full of long hair waiting to be turned into wigs.

Bella started to tell the story of the factory. "I was so delighted when Alfred suggested that we move to Oregon. I'm not sure why, but as I look back, I realize it was my destiny. And as my destiny, it also became the destiny of my family."

She explained, "Alfred and I moved here when Aurelia was nine. She missed so many things about New York, but being young, she adapted better than I did. After we were here several months and our beautiful new house was taking shape, Alfred caught me in a blue mood one day. He asked what I missed most about New York. It so happens what I missed the most was my friends. The women of Monteith looked at me like an oddity, a big city woman who thought she was too good for them. That couldn't have been farther from the truth though. I so longed for the companionship of other women."

"That was when I got the idea to open the wig factory. Oh, I know Alfred thought I was off my rocker, but he would have let me have anything. When the town heard about the factory, they thought it was the craziest idea in the whole world. In fact, on more than one occasion, I overheard it referred to as 'The Wacky Willamette Wig Factory.' No one said anything to me though. Partially because they were wonderful people and partially because building the factory kept them employed, at a very nice wage, for several months."

"Gradually, more and more of the town's women talked to me during the construction. They were intrigued and all around curious about what the Willamette Valley was going to do with a wig factory." She winked, "Although I think they were secretly delighted at the thought of such a big city notion coming to their small town."

Bella's whole audience listened in rapt attention, even Aurelia and Athena who had heard the story many times before. After all, this was their heritage and their legacy. It was now Willy's heritage and legacy as well.

Bella continued, "It turns out I made some wonderful friends before the factory even opened. Once a few of the women talked to me, everyone seemed to want to get to know me. I was in heaven! Then construction on the factory finished and I was ready to get going. The day I had the idea to open the wig factory, I started sending letters to my friends in New York. I told them I was going to need a master wig craftsman to come to Monteith and teach the people I hired how to craft wearable works of art."

"My dear friend, Porscha Vanderhoogen, found the perfect man for the job. His name was Alexander Thoreau. She wrote to me that he would be arriving in Monteith on July thirtieth and he had already taken care of ordering all the supplies we would need to get started. All I needed to do was to staff my factory. Initially, I found three women who very much wanted to learn the art of wig making. The hitch was all three of these ladies had young children who weren't in school yet. That was when I had the idea to turn the third floor into a nursery. I hired Leticia Kringle to watch the children. She was seventy-one-years old and loved the idea of being needed. The children adored her too. It was the ideal situation."

Willy asked, "Aunt Bella, I don't mean to

interrupt, but it seems like you were spending a lot of money. Did this place ever make money?"

"Oh my, yes. Once we all got going and figured out what we were doing, I sent three of our creations to Porscha to thank her for finding Alexander. Well, let me tell you, the Vanderhoogens were a very big deal in New York society and Porscha loved the wigs we sent so much that she wore them everywhere. We were getting orders from society ladies up and down Fifth and Park Avenues. Then Porscha took her wigs with her to Europe and told all her friends abroad about them. Her friends told their friends and on and on it went. The Willamette Wig Factory became a very big deal, indeed." She added, "We always had a thriving business here. Unfortunately, we let our poor Georgie down by getting old and dying. We left her all alone. That is why we had come back to help her."

Tommy said, "But Mrs. C. is pretty old herself. Why did you wait so long?"

Bella replied, "Tommy dear, life is about learning. We all learn from our mistakes, but sometimes we need a helping hand to see that we've even made mistakes. We were hoping Georgie would realize her error all by herself. When she didn't, we were sent back to help her."

Tommy wasn't quite done with her questions,

"Who exactly sent you here?"

Bella answered her, "Don't be obtuse Tommy dear. I happen to know that your families are good Presbyterians. Try paying closer attention in church, hmmm?"

"So you're saying God's Presbyterian?"

"Dear, God isn't any particular religion. We are all his children and we are all his creation. Now, if you will please quit getting off track, we have some more work to do here."

The five ladies continued to fine hone the details of phase two and the more they talked, the more certain they were that The Willamette Wig Factory was definitely going to re-open as planned. Willy and Tommy forgot all about asking who the boy on the carousel was.

Execution

Executing phase two was going to take a bit of time. Bella said they had to go slow and make Georgianna think reopening the factory was her own idea. For that reason, the five schemers decided to wait a full week before meeting again. In the meantime Willy and Tommy had a lot to accomplish, so they got to work immediately. The next morning they woke bright and early and started their plan. They decided to go see Mrs. C. first and try to convince her to join them in a little shopping expedition.

Mrs. Carbunkle was delighted when her young friends showed up at her front door. She complimented Willy on what a nice job she was doing taking care of her wig and she told Tommy the black fringe was really growing on her. Then she invited them in for tea and maple syrup muffins. Willy and Tommy could not pass up any of Mrs. C.'s baked goods, so they happily went inside to satisfy their stomachs and talk Mrs. C. into going to town with them. It turns out they didn't have to work too hard to convince her.

Mrs. C. had such a nice time going out with the girls the day before she was more than eager to join them. She even wanted to stop into The Clothes Horse and buy herself a new cardigan. Mrs. C. grabbed her purse and cane, just in case her legs got tired. The girls each grabbed an extra muffin and off they went.

Willy and Tommy left their bikes at Mrs. C.'s house and the three friends strolled toward First Street at a slow crawl. Willy was amazed by how many more things she noticed by walking versus riding her bike. For instance, she never realized how amazing wisteria vines smelled up close. She secretly decided she was very happy living in Oregon with her great new friend Tommy and her new relative, Mrs. Carbunkle. Life was certainly a whole lot more interesting here in Monteith than it had ever been in Mason.

The ladies arrived at The Clothes Horse at exactly nine a.m. They were standing at the front door when Miss Bickle unlocked it. Willy had never been inside the store before and from what she saw she wouldn't be back anytime soon, unless she was with Mrs. C. of course. The clothes were very grandmotherly, cardigans and orthopedic shoes as far as the eye could see. Talk about a small town fashion crisis. Actually, she thought, this was going to fit right into phase two.

Willy said to Tommy, loud enough so Mrs. C. could hear, "Shoot, Tommy, that poor Miss Bickle has the frumpiest hair, doesn't she? I don't think I've ever seen such a messed up style."

Tommy caught on right away, "I know what you mean, Willy. It's a shame really. But wait until you meet Belinda Smoot at the pharmacy. She's a hot mess!"

Mrs. C. was listening to her young friends with a frown on her face, "Girls, that is no way to talk about the lovely ladies of Monteith. I'm surprised at both of you. I thought you had better manners than that."

Uh, oh, where was this going? Mrs. C. wasn't listening to the meat of the conversation. Willy tried to assure her they weren't trying to be nasty, it was just that they felt bad for these ladies. Willy didn't know how far she could push it, but she decided to try just a little more. "What I meant, Mrs. C., is that after seeing all those wonderful wigs the other day, I guess I just realized how boring people look without them. You know, the ladies of the Willamette Valley must have really been glamorous once upon a time."

Mrs. C. looked at Willy like she wasn't quite sure if she was being played or not. She decided to ignore her young friend for a moment and try on a bright red cardigan. Willy and Tommy made eye contact and shrugged their shoulders. They weren't quite sure where to go from there. Tommy told Mrs. C. that she looked like a fashion plate in red and then added, "Too bad poor Miss Bickle doesn't."

"Thomasina Andretti, that's enough of that! If you keep gossiping about Elsie Bickle, she's going to hear you and she's just about the sweetest lady in town. Now you girls go over there and pick out a nice pair of walking shoes for me in a size six. I'll be right over to try them on." Willy and Tommy went over to the shoes. As they weren't in the least bit in jeopardy of finding a nice pair of shoes, they chose the least ugly. Keeping in mind, they were still plenty ugly. Mrs. C. came over, tried them on, declared they were gorgeous and bought both the shoes and the red sweater.

The next stop was the pharmacy. Mrs. C. sternly reminded the girls that under pain of death, they were not to talk about Belinda Smoot's hair while they were there. The girls weren't sure if they had already ruined phase two by making Mrs. C. mad. So they decided to quiet down for a while. What they didn't realize was Mrs. C. had already started to see everyone's hair for what it really was. She thought poor Elsie Bickle did look a fright and sweet heaven, was Belinda's hair frosted? When had the town taken such a turn for the worse?

The final stop of the morning was a trip to The Plucky Pig for iced tea and French fries. Mrs. C. didn't think she needed any fries but once they arrived, they ate them so fast they ordered more. While waiting for the second order to arrive, Bree Petersen walked in. She was all alone without her nasty side-kick. Bree saw the girls and headed right over to them. Tommy rolled her eyes and mumbled under her breath, "Here we go again."

Bree approached the table and politely greeted Tommy and Mrs. C. Then she focused her attention on Willy and apologized. "Willy, I am so sorry about what Tiffany said about your hair the other day. I felt just awful. It isn't in the least common or trashy. It's very pretty." Then she added, "I hope you don't think I was a part of tripping you at the pool either. That was all Tiff's idea."

Willy and Tommy were both stunned. Would wonders never cease?

Willy smiled, "Thanks Bree, that's really nice of you. I was hoping I hadn't made two enemies so soon after moving here."

Bree smiled, "I'd actually like to be your friend. I

don't care what Tiffany says. She's getting harder and harder to be friends with. I just feel so rotten after a day of listening to her complain about everyone."

Tommy was struck with a fabulous idea and asked Bree to meet them at her house at two o'clock that afternoon. That would give Willy and her and enough time to get Mrs. C. home in one piece and then get back to her house to set her side plan into motion.

Mrs. C. listened to the whole conversation intently and only seemed to hear one part of it. After Bree left, she demanded, "Wilhelmina, who thought your hair was trashy and common? I want a name!"

Willy and Tommy were a little surprised by Mrs. C.'s outburst. They told her all about Tiffany and her rotten comments about Willy's hair. Mrs. C. listened quietly and thought to herself, the Willamette Valley really was in trouble if anyone could ever think Wilhelmina's gorgeous new wig was trashy. What had happened to her town? She would have to think on this and see if she could come up with a solution.

Revenge

Revenge is sweet. After dropping Mrs. C. off, Tommy told Willy all about her side plan. Willy liked it but wasn't too sure it was the right thing to do. After all, they were just trying to get the factory reopened. They weren't supposed to hurt anyone. To which Tommy said, "Hurt? What hurt? No one's getting hurt here. We're just proving the old adage that what goes around, comes around. And sometimes it needs a little help coming around." She smiled, "That's where we come in."

Willy listened to the plan again, quietly thought about it and then started to laugh.

She declared, "Tommy, you're right. If I can move here all the way from Illinois *and* cut my hair, all to get a factory open again, I think that putting your plan into motion is the least Tiffany can do to help the cause. Let's start looking through magazines and come up with the right picture."

Tommy retrieved a stack of old magazines from Charlie's room and the two friends poured through them for ages. They just couldn't find the right look though. That was when Tommy got another idea. She said to Willy, "Come on, follow me into my mom's room. I just remembered she's got the perfect photo in one of her old modeling portfolios."

The girls went into Mr. and Mrs. Andretti's bedroom and Tommy pulled out a bunch of leather portfolios from under the bed.

"Here, start looking in these. You'll get more ideas than you thought possible."

Ginger Andretti was a famous model in the eighties and the cover of all of her old portfolios had a name embossed on each of them.

Willy gasped, "Tommy, do these say what I think they say?"

Tommy laughed, "They sure do! They all say 'Wilhelmina.' My mom was with the Wilhelmina modeling agency in New York." She added, "It's one of the best agencies in the world, named after some famous model, Wilhelmina something or other."

Willy was astounded by this news. There was a famous model named Wilhelmina who opened her own agency? Not only that, but it was one of the best agencies in the world? Wow, this was an empowering moment. Willy started to like her name a bit more.

The girls started flipping through the portfolios looking for just the right photograph.

Willy sighed, "Jeez, Tommy, your mom was gorgeous. She doesn't look anything like a mom."

Tommy answered, "It's really cool, but she's just my mom, so I don't normally think of her like this, you know? I mean, you see what she looks like when she runs around here."

The girls continued to flip through page after page. There were ads for shampoo and well-known make-up lines and famous designers. Willy finally picked up the portfolio from the mid-eighties and shrieked, "Holy cow, these are scary!"

Tommy knew that her friend had just found the portfolio they needed. She answered, "I don't know what to tell ya, Will. The eighties were a really freaky time for hair fashions. I told my mom that and she just laughed. She said they all thought they were so glamorous then. She told me about some kind of style called 'The Flock of Seagulls' look. She said if I wanted to see awful, I should find a picture of that. Hey, do you think we should go on line and see if we can find one?"

Willy answered, "If it's any worse than this one right here, I'm gonna have to say no. I mean, there's getting even and then there's just plain cruel." She pointed to a particular picture and said, "I think this one is bad enough."

The photo Willy was holding was of Ginger with long hair and about two million layers cut into it. The top of her hair was styled with gel and sprung out all over her head like she had just been hit by lightening. She had on a really short black dress that was ripped all over and she was wearing enormous earrings while playing a guitar. Man, what some people thought of as stylish!

Willy and Tommy decided to use that picture just as the doorbell rang. Bree had arrived. They went downstairs to let her in and then took her up to Tommy's bedroom to discuss the plan. Willy was nervous that Bree would think it was too mean but Bree laughed so hard she started to cry. She was convinced it was a great payback.

Bree took right off for Tiff's house. She said she wanted to stay and get to know Willy better, but there would be plenty of time to do that after their little revenge scheme. Twenty-seven minutes later, Bree called Tommy to let her know the plan had been set in motion. She said they would be over the next morning at eleven a.m. If everything went on schedule, they would meet at Mrs. C.'s around two. In less than twenty-four hours, life was going to be a whole heck of a lot more interesting in Monteith

11 A.M.

First thing the next morning, Tommy filled Charlie in on the details of her plan. After all, Charlie's cooperation was essential for its success. Tommy told her sister only about a third of what had been going on in her life. She couldn't tell her everything because she had promised to keep the factory and the plan to reopen it a secret. Tommy showed her sister the picture of their mom and waited. Charlie finally said, "Kid, I always told you that you were smart, but this level of scheming is a little frightening." Then she laughed, "But, if this Tiffany girl is really such an obnoxious brat, I'm in."

Excellent! Now Tommy just had to wait for the doorbell to ring, which it did approximately twelve minutes later. Tiffany was wearing her long blonde hair in a very sleek and classic ponytail. Tommy silently admired it, thinking it would be perfect for a hair commercial. She would have felt bad for Tiffany if she weren't so shallow and mean, but the cheerleader wasn't nice and consequently was about to get exactly what she deserved.

Tommy greeted, "Hey, guys, come on in. I'm so glad you came over."

Tiffany was a little leery of Tommy's enthusiasm after her behavior at The Plucky Pig, but she went in anyway. She smiled, "Hi, Tommy, I was really happy when Bree said she ran into you and you invited us over today. I was kind of surprised actually."

"Well, Tiff, I got to thinking about what you said about my mom helping you with finding your perfect hairstyle and I think you might be on to something."

Tiffany looked around, "Is your mom here? Is she going to help me?"

"Sorry Tiff, she has a bull riding class today, but she left me with some great ideas." Tommy asked, "You know we just got back from New York, right? Well, when we were there, my mom went into the city to see her old modeling agent and I guess the agency was a total zoo. Franz La Bonge was in town from Paris and he was cutting all of the models hair in the latest style."

Tiffany excitedly asked, "What new style? I've been reading all the magazines and I haven't seen anything about a new style."

Tommy snorted, "What do the magazines know?

They don't know what's new until the models show them. The new look will be in all the magazines by next month." She added, "You know how the seventies came back into fashion a while ago? Well the eighties are next. My mom was so excited that she had Franz cut her hair and they asked her to do a photo shoot for next month's Vogue. Can you stand it? It was so cool! Vogue got all the supermodels from the eighties together and shot them with their new retro hairdos."

Tiff declared, "That's awesome! I can't wait for the pictures to come out. As soon as the issue is on the newsstands, I'm going to buy it and have Sheila McNut down at The Hair Hutch give me the same cut your mom got. I can hardly wait!"

Tommy cut her off, "That's the best part, Tiff. You don't have to wait. I have a picture from the shoot. Come on up to my room and I'll show it to you."

Tommy, Tiffany and Bree ran right up to Tommy's room for the grand unveiling. All three girls were very excited, for different reasons of course. Tommy couldn't wait to get even at Tiffany for her nasty comments to Willy. Bree couldn't wait to bring Tiff down a few notches and Tiff couldn't wait because she was going to get her hair done long before the new trend hit Monteith. That would show everyone how much better she was than they were. She might even win Jamie back.

Tommy brought out the picture and showed the other two girls. It was all she could do not to laugh. Tiffany looked shocked but didn't say anything right away. Bree announced, "That is the coolest hair I've EVER seen! Tommy, your mom looks terrific! I'm going to start growing my hair out just so I can get it done like this."

Tommy sighed, "I know what you mean, Bree. I've got to let mine grow at least four inches before I can do it, three for length and one so I can cut the black fringe off the bottom of my hair."

Tiff piped in, "You poor girls. I guess I'm the only one who can do it now."

"Yeah," Tommy said, "But Tiff, don't you think it's a little too sophisticated for you? I mean it's such a hot trend. Someone like my mom could pull it off, but do you really think you could?"

"Of course I can! I've got the same color hair as your mom and the same length and more than one person has told me I'd be a perfect model. I just wish Sheila McNut wasn't booked so far in advance, otherwise I'd get it done today."

Tommy was having a hard time keeping a straight face, "Just think how hard it's going to be to get an appointment with her once the new magazines come out."

Tommy went on to say it was too bad Tiffany didn't like Willy's hair because Charlie was the one that cut it for her and she was always available. Tiffany didn't want to tell Tommy how pretty she thought Willy's hair really was and Tommy certainly wasn't going to tell Tiff that Willy was wearing a wig and that her real haircut was a nightmare. This was getting very complicated. Tiffany finally said, "You know Tommy, it's not like Charlie could really do anything with that red mop. I'd be willing to let her do my hair, if she's around."

Tommy had to keep herself from jumping up and screaming for her sister. Instead she got up slowly, shrugged her shoulders and answered, "I don't know if she's even home right now, but I'll go take a look."

Tommy walked out of the room and ran down the hall to get Charlie to let her know the plan was a go. Charlie said she'd set up her bathroom and would be ready in two minutes. Tommy went to deliver the good news to Tiff.

Tiff screamed in excitement, "Oh my gosh, I can hardly believe it. Today, I'm going to become a model! Move over girls, I'm on my way!"

If Tommy had been feeling the least little bit sorry for Tiff, she wasn't now. In fact, now she wanted to dye her hair purple, too. The girls went into the bathroom to begin Tiff's transformation. Charlie sat the snooty cheerleader down on the toilet seat and started chopping great chunks out of her hair. Tiff didn't seem to notice or care, but Bree and Tommy were looking a little green around the gills. There was no going back now. After forty minutes, Charlie was finished with her masterpiece. Not that anyone would have thought it was possible, but she made Tiff's hair look even worse than the picture. Yet in Tiffany's eyes it looked even better.

Tiff couldn't wait to walk around town and show everyone how fabulous she looked. She decided that she would be just in time to catch the lunch rush at The Plucky Pig. Tiffany, Bree and Tommy left the house to show Monteith that a star was born. Tommy could hardly wait. They would have at least an hour of Tiff preening at the diner before Willy was scheduled to show up with Mrs. Carbunkle. This little act of revenge had killed two birds with one stone. Tiffany would get a taste of what it was like having others talk about her and Mrs. Carbunkle would see yet another atrocious hairstyle in the Willamette Valley. If this one wasn't enough to get her to reopen the factory, she figured the factory would remain abandoned forever.

The Willamette Valley Is A Long Way From New York

The Willamette Valley was a long way from New York. What may have been all the rage in New York was liable to get you laughed out of a town like Monteith, not to mention, what was considered fashionable in New York in the eighties. The models wore so much heavy make-up that Tommy's mom actually looked younger now than she did in some of her modeling shots that were nearly thirty-years old.

Tommy, Bree, and Tiffany were getting ready to head out to show off Tiff's new look to the town when Tiff was struck by a brilliant idea. If the new hairstyle was all the rage, what about her clothes? Tommy had never even thought about that. But leave it to Tiff. She wanted to be one hundred percent solid, authentic, in the latest fashion. So, with Charlie's assistance, Tiffany became a creature out of a horror flick. Charlie had an old black dress that she was happy to mutilate for the cause. She took the picture of her mom and made a "mini-me" out of Tiff. Tiff ended up looking so scary that Tommy and Bree tried to get her to change her mind about the dress and just show off her hair. But the more they tried to talk her out of it, the more she wanted it.

Tommy even begged, "Don't wear the dress yet, Tiff. I'm not sure Oregon is ready for it."

To which Tiffany demanded, "How can I show everyone how small town and backwards they are if I don't give them the *whole* new look?" She decided, "They really are fortunate to have women like me and your mom in town to show them what real fashion looks like."

There it was again. Tiffany's attitude made it impossible to save her from herself. She was bound and determined to make this little lesson in humility a real whopper. Tommy started to feel like Dr. Frankenstein and Tiff was her monster.

With the time it took to get Tiff dressed, they were going to miss the big rush at the diner, but Tommy was actually glad for that now. The girls took off on their bikes and got to The Plucky Pig by a quarter after one. Tiff almost caused three car accidents on the way as people were watching her and not the road. She was perfectly aware that everyone was staring at her and she was enjoying every moment of it.

When they finally got to the diner, Tiffany's grand entrance was like something out of a movie. As soon as she walked in, the entire restaurant went dead quiet. A couple of people dropped their silverware and jaws hung open like flycatchers. Tiffany gave everyone a beatific smile and then proceeded to do her version of a model's cat-walk all the way over to a booth in the corner. But instead of looking like a sophisticated model, she wound up looking like she had just dislocated a hip.

Once the girls were settled, Mr. Jim, the owner of The Plucky Pig, came over and took their order. He greeted, "Hey girls," then asked, "Tiff, you working on your Halloween costume already?"

The cheerleader looked at Mr. Jim like he was the biggest bumpkin in the whole world and sneered, "Mr. Jim, I certainly don't expect *you* to know what is going on in the world of fashion, but this is the next biggest craze coming out of New York City."

Mr. Jim rolled his eyes and mumbled something like it must be the new craze with the loonies at the Bedlam home for the mentally ill. Then he took the girls' orders and set out to let the other locals know Tiffany purposely dressed herself in an attempt to copy some wild new fashion.

Monteith, being a small town without a whole heck of a lot going on, was very aware of anything new and interesting happening in town. As a matter of fact, one night, the president of the bank's wife, Mrs. Bolenbloom fell asleep on her bed while her bathtub was filling with water. She nodded off with the faucet running and woke up at two-thirty in the morning to a huge crash. The crash was the bathtub falling through the floor and landing on the dining room table. Before Mrs. Bolenbloom could even get out of bed to investigate, her phone started to ring. It was Trina Ettlesman calling to say that she just heard about Mrs. Bolenbloom's bathtub and if she needed anything, to just call. The Bolenblooms had just moved to the Willamette Valley from Chicago, a city where no one knew your business unless you told them. Needless to say, Mrs. Bolenbloom was ready to move back. What unnerved her even more was that her husband, who was out of town on business, called her at seven o'clock the next morning to say that *he'd* just heard about the tub!

Now, if it took less than ten seconds for the town to hear about the Bolenbloom's bath tub in the middle of the night, imagine how long it would take for them to be gossiping about Tiff and her "new look," in the middle of the day, in the middle of a crowded diner.

While Tommy, Bree and Charlie were taking care of Tiff, Willy was visiting with Mrs. C. She went to her house at ten-thirty that morning. The two new friends had a wonderful chat about their mutual relatives. Then, at about one o'clock, Willy suggested they go out for a little walk. Mrs. C. thought that was a marvelous idea. She claimed to have felt so refreshed after her exercise the day before that she couldn't wait to stretch her legs again. The truth was that Mrs. C. was only marginally interested in the exercise. She was more curious to get a good look at the women of Monteith. Now that her eyes had been opened and she had started to pay attention to their hair again, she was ready to see how bad things had really gotten. So after a long stroll through town, Willy and Mrs. C. walked into the diner at one forty-five on the nose.

When they arrived, the whole place was buzzing like a hive of hyperactive bees. Mrs. C. told Willy that someone was definitely up to something. This was a buzzing she hadn't heard since the day Mrs. Bolenbloom's bathtub fell in.

Mrs. C. and Willy sat at a table by the window. That's when Mrs. C. realized the source of the commotion. She asked Willy if she knew who the frightening looking girl was that was sitting with

Tommy. Willy told her all about Tiffany, reminding her that Tiffany was the one who thought that Willy's hair was common and trashy. After hearing that, Mrs. C. pulled herself up and marched right over to Tiffany's table.

She demanded, "Thomasina dear, I need to speak with you. Will you please join me at my table?"

Tommy agreed and followed Mrs.C. through the diner without uttering a word. Once they'd both sat down, Mrs. C. took a deep breath and asked, "Thomasina Andretti, why are you here with that dreadful, dreadful girl?"

Tommy answered, "Oh Mrs. C., I'm not here with her. I just stopped in for an iced tea and there she was. I just went over to find out why she looked the way she did."

"And why in the name of all that is holy, does she look like that?"

"Well, Mrs. C., she says it's the new style and that in a matter of months, all of Monteith is going to be getting their hair done like that."

Mrs. Carbunkle stood up and exclaimed, "Dears, let's go. We haven't a moment to lose!"

Willy asked, "Where are we going Mrs. C.?"

"We are going to the factory. We have to clean it from stem to stern. We need to find a wig designer and we need to hire some staff. The Willamette Wig

Factory is going to open for business again. This valley NEEDS me!"

With great big smiles on their faces, the two girls each grabbed one of Mrs. C.'s hands and like the three musketeers they took off down First Street with a spring in their step. Phase two was a success!

Preparation

Getting the factory ready to reopen was going to be a lot of work. Willy and Tommy wondered how two young girls and one old lady would be able to clean and organize the entire building. The answer was actually quite elementary. In reality, there would be four girls, one old lady and one much younger lady. The girls had completely forgotten about Bella, Aurelia and Athena.

On the way to the factory, Mrs. C. and her young friends stopped at The Clean Machine to pick up wood soap, brass cleaner, and about seventy-five other cleaning supplies they'd need. They were dragging under the weight of their purchases by the time they got back to the little alley off Walnut.

Mrs. C. was so intent on getting inside the factory she didn't even notice that the outside of the factory looked positively wonderful! The ivy had been pruned back, the door freshly polished, and the window boxes were full of brilliantly colored flowers. The girls realized their ghost friends had been hard at work. They were just about to follow Mrs. C. into the factory when their attention was once again drawn to the old carousel. After putting their purchases down, they slowly walked toward the decrepit machine.

Willy whispered, "Look, there's that boy again."

Her friend uttered, "I have absolutely no idea who he is. He looks like he's about our age but I've never seen him before."

As the girls approached the fence blocking the entrance to the ruins, they saw the boy waving to them. He was sitting on the carousel's rabbit holding a tattered book.

Willy called out, "Hi! What are you doing here?"

He smiled, "Just hanging out on my favorite animal."

Tommy interjected, "You know it's dangerous in there. That's the whole reason they built a fence."

The boy replied, "I'm okay. I won't get hurt." With a wink, he added, "I promise."

Willy asked, "What's your name? Do you go to school in Monteith?"

He answered, "My name's Bobby. I used to go to school here, but not anymore."

Tommy wondered, "When did you move? I don't

remember ever seeing you before."

Without really answering her question he answered, "I come back once in a while to see if the town ever decided to restore this old thing." With a longing look, he added, "My mom and I used to come here every Saturday and dream of how we could raise enough money to bring the carousel back to life."

Willy asked, "Where's your mom now?"

Tommy added, "Yeah, does she know you're risking life and limb crawling around that broken-down old thing?"

Bobby answered, "The answer to the first question is, she's in town running errands. And the answer to the second is that she doesn't know I'm in here." With a wink, he added, "Let's keep that our little secret, okay?"

Tommy snapped, "Oh sure, we'll keep it a secret. What do you want us to do when the whole thing collapses under you and we can't get in to help you? Should we just walk away and leave you there?"

Bobby laughed, "If it collapses, you have my permission to leave me. Deal?"

Despite feeling irritated that this kid was risking his life, Tommy smiled, "Fine, it's a deal. You kill yourself in there and we'll pretend we didn't see a thing."

Willy interrupted, "Tommy, we need to get back to the factory and help Mrs. C."

"Holy beans, you're right." Then to Bobby, Tommy said, "We need to get going, but maybe we'll see you around some time."

Bobby waved, "I'll be here. See you later." Then he went back to reading his book.

As the friends walked away, Willy said, "I get the feeling Bobby wants to live on the old carousel."

Tommy laughed, "Good luck with that, huh? His mom will eventually find him and drag him off."

Once the girls stepped back over the threshold of the factory, they were in nonstop motion. Mrs. Carbunkle filled buckets of soapy water for them. They started scrubbing down the staircase while Mrs. C. went through the yellow pages to locate a painter, plumber and handyman. Willy and Tommy were happily working on the stairs when they noticed Bella, Aurelia and Athena cleaning the windows in the sitting room. Mrs. C. didn't notice them, but her three ghostly relatives were busily working along side the rest of them to get the factory ready.

As the phone hadn't been turned on yet and Mrs. C. didn't own a cell phone, she told the girls she would have to walk home to make some calls. She vowed to be back soon and promised to bring lunch, since they left the diner before actually eating. Once

Mrs. Carbunkle left, Bella, Aurelia and Athena approached Willy and Tommy to praise them on their wonderful execution of phase two. Bella confessed that she particularly liked the bit with Tiffany's hair. Having admitted that, she warned them they would eventually have to make it up to their classmate. Then she abruptly excused herself, citing other things she had to do. Most importantly, she had to help her Georgie find a new wig artisan and she needed to solve that little problem immediately.

In the meantime, Mrs. Carbunkle went home and made her calls. She hired Brody Beasley and his crew to paint, Arnold Ship to do the plumbing and Bernard Potts for various repairs. Once she was done she realized the chandeliers would have to be cleaned, so she called LaVonda Tremaine over at Diabolical Cleaners and asked her to send three women to come and polish them for her. What next? Oh, of course, how could she have forgotten? They needed a new wig designer. Well, how in heaven's green pastures was she going to find someone for that job? She would just have to think about it. But first, she would make some sandwiches and get back to the girls.

When Mrs. C. returned to the factory, she discovered her young friends sitting in the front room with a rather odd looking young man. The stranger was wearing an old fashioned cut-away coat and a bow tie. His hair was so blond it was almost white and his face made him look like he was no more than a schoolboy. When he noticed Mrs. C., he immediately leaped up and introduced himself as Broadwyn Banister. He informed her that he had grown up hearing his grandmother talk about The Willamette Wig Factory. He explained that his great, great, great, uncle Alexander Thoreau, used to design all the wigs for the factory when it first opened. Mrs. Carbunkle had to grab the back of a Queen Anne chair to keep from falling over in surprise. What an unexpected and timely visit!

Mrs. C. excitedly inquired, "Broadwyn dear, you aren't by any chance a wig designer yourself, are you?"

Broadwyn smiled brilliantly, "Why yes, Mrs. Carbunkle, I am. In fact I've just come from a seminar on modern wig designs in Portland. I'm on my way to visit my grandmother and I thought I'd stop by The Willamette Wig Factory to see where my ancestor worked."

"Dear, you aren't by any chance looking for a position, are you?"

Broadwyn, confessed that he wasn't, but was curious where this was going. So he replied, "I already have a very good job with "Haute Hair" in New York. What exactly is it you're offering?"

Mrs. C. explained to Broadwyn the story of how she closed the factory and proceeded to explain why she absolutely must reopen it. She confessed that she didn't know what the going rate was for a wig designer, but declared that she would be more than happy to match his current salary and even give him a share in the profits. She offered to start looking at houses for him to rent and further sweetened the deal by promising to make him all the baked goods he could eat, if he took the job that is.

Broadwyn had never considered leaving New York City before, but the chance to work at the same factory as his illustrious ancestor was just too tempting an offer to pass up. He vowed that after he visited with his grandmother, he would fly back to New York, pack up his apartment and be back in Monteith in a mere four weeks. He even suggested that one or two of his fellow workers might be persuaded to come with him. They sealed their deal with a hug and then toasted it with milk and cookies. After Broadwyn left for his visit with his grandmother they all got back to work.

In the span of one afternoon, almost all of the kinks in reopening the factory had been worked out. Tommy and Willy had agreed to work in the shop during the summer and help out during the school year. It was Mrs. C.'s idea to ask Tommy's sister, Charlie to work there as well. So the entire factory had been staffed in the course of ten minutes. If that wasn't a sign The Willamette Wig Factory was meant to be, what was?

The ladies wrapped up work at five p.m. That is, Willy, Tommy, and Mrs. C. stopped working. Bella, Aurelia and Athena kept going long into the night. Tommy and Willy grabbed their bikes and rode to the Andretti's to tell Charlie about the great new job they had for her. Mrs. C. went home to bake cookies. She couldn't remember having ever been so happy in her life. She swore she could almost feel her mother and grandmother around. Now if that wasn't a fanciful notion.

Onward And Upward

In the next two days, Willy, Tommy, Mrs. C. and Charlie turned the factory into a sparkling edifice. The ladies from Diabolical Cleaners did a beautiful job on the chandeliers. Brody Beasley and his crew had begun painting and Arnold Ship was working hard on updating the plumbing. Broadwyn Banister called and said he had talked to a few of his friends from Haute Hair into joining him. They would be arriving in Monteith with him. He also explained that he went ahead and ordered supplies that would be delivered within the next couple of weeks. Tommy heard that and thought she'd expire from anticipation. She couldn't wait to see the wonderful creations Broadwyn and his crew would come up with. She decided to wear a new wig every day once they were open for business.

Charlie was really getting into the excitement, too. It was her idea to turn the sitting room into a coffee bar. They would serve coffee, tea and hot chocolate. They would also sell Mrs. Carbunkle's cookies and muffins that she would make right there in the factory's kitchen. They even decided to order some goodies from some of the town's best bakers. No one made lemon bars like Delia Banks and Viola Fritz made the best rhubarb coffee cake. Charlie thought because the ladies of Monteith hadn't worn wigs in so long it might take them a little time to get back into the swing of things. But with a new coffee bar, she knew they would definitely come to check out the factory.

Mrs. Carbunkle thought it was an excellent idea. She confided to Willy and Tommy she was just a little worried that all the new things for the coffee bar might break or disappear though. She reminded them about the days when Aurelia and Athena tried to make additions. But regardless of the past, she was willing to give it a try.

That afternoon, while Willy was in the ladies' room, Bella popped in to tell her she, Aurelia and Athena loved the idea of the coffee bar. She told Willy not to worry about things breaking either. She also informed Willy it was time for her to let Georgie know they were related. Bella thought the best way to do this would be for her to tell Mrs. C. she was going through her family bible and found out she had a great, great, great, great aunt named Bella. Willy was to explain her aunt was named Bella Bennet, though, not Bella Barnes, like Mrs. C.'s relative. Mrs. C. would immediately realize there was a connection between the two of them. Bella said after Georgie figured out about the connection, Willy should tell her parents, too.

So Willy told Mrs. C. about her great, great, great, great aunt. Mrs. C. recognized the name immediately and burst into tears. She knew Willy was special the day she met her and now she knew why. The Snodgrass's were just as tickled to learn they had a relative in town and were very excited to learn more of their family history.

The next couple of weeks progressed very nicely. Mrs. C. bought four antique ice-cream tables with matching chairs at Goodwill. Willy and Tommy scrubbed them down, sanded off the old paint and refinished them. The sofa and chairs in the sitting room were moved against the walls. Little tables were placed by them so people could sit and enjoy their coffee and cookies. The new tables were situated in the center of the sitting room. The whole effect was magical and when it was all completed, it looked like a tearoom from 1889. The only new thing that had broken was a teacup and the only reason it shattered was because Tommy dropped it.

Mrs. C. printed flyers telling the residents of Monteith the wig factory was going to reopen. The flyers announced the new coffee bar and the fact The Annex would be open for business as well. The ladies of Monteith could borrow any wig for free for the first month. After that, for a one-time fee, they could purchase a wig ticket that would allow them to continue to use any creation The Annex had to offer.

While Willy and Tommy were goofing off in the kitchen one day, Bella startled them by materializing out of thin air. Once again she praised them for all their hard work and affirmed how proud she was of them. She also mentioned she knew Tiffany was still running around town in her "new" look. She thought it was time for the girls to tell her the truth. There was no new look coming out in Vogue.

Amends

Wasn't it Newton's law of physics that said, "For every action, there is an equal and opposite reaction?" That is exactly what Willy and Tommy were discovering. For as much fun as it was to mess with Tiffany, it was going to be at least that hard to tell her the truth. If it was up to them, they would have never come clean, but they were hardly going to ignore Bella's dictate.

Tommy called Tiffany and asked if she could come over to her house. Tiffany was glad that Tommy called. She had been wondering why the new look hadn't shown up in the latest issue of Vogue. Tommy assured her that's what she wanted to talk to her about and promised to explain everything when she got there. On the way to Tiffany's house, Willy and Tommy stopped by the factory to pick up a peace offering for Tiff. They went into the storage room and searched the labels on all the boxes until they found "long, wheat blonde with sunlit highlights." They opened the box to make sure that it was the right color and found the same problem that Willy had with her wig. There was way too much hair and there was no shape to it at all. What were they going to do? After they agonized for a good fifteen minutes, Athena finally appeared in the room.

Willy said, "Thank goodness, Athena. Is there any chance you can style this into something fabulous?"

Athena nodded, "There is every chance that I can. That's why I'm here."

Tommy gave her a side long look and asked, "Is there any reason you didn't show up sooner?"

"Of course."

Tommy continued, "Might you share it with us?"

"Of course Tommy, Grandmother, Mother and I were enjoying your discomfort. We thought perhaps if you had to worry a bit you might not be so hasty in pulling a prank like this again. Do you think that might be true?"

"First of all, you guys are really mean. I thought you were angels or something. Secondly, I suppose it's true. But now that you've taught me this lesson, would you mind cutting the wig already?"

"I wouldn't mind at all Tommy. Would you be so good as to put it on for me? That will help me greatly in styling it."

Tommy put the wig on and in short order Athena turned it into the most gorgeous hairstyle that either girl had ever seen. Tommy exclaimed, "Athena, this is amazing! I would love to have a wig like this. Any chance you might cut one for me too?"

Athena declared, "No. I think Tiffany should enjoy being the only one to have this particular hairstyle. I think she's paid the price, don't you?" She added, "Don't fret though, I have a particular style in mind for you and I'll cut it for you before the grand opening."

Tommy was somewhat mollified by that declaration. Willy grabbed an extra foam wig head out of the storage closet and put the wig and head in a bag. Then the girls said goodbye to Athena and went off to meet their destiny.

Tiffany opened the door shortly after they knocked and was very surprised to see Willy there. She looked at Tommy and demanded, "What is *she* doing here?"

"Tiff, can we please come in?"

Tiffany stepped aside, looking none too happy and conceded, "I suppose."

Tommy and Willy went into Tiffany's living room. They cringed to see that Tiff was still doing her hair the same way. They decided that she must have been purchasing gel by the gallon.

Tommy started, "Tiff, I've got to tell you something and you're just going to have to sit there and hear me out." Tiff silently sat down and Tommy continued, "First off, you are a *very* nasty person. I'm sorry if that hurts your feelings, but it's true. You seem to go out of your way to say horrible things about other people, all the time. But when you turned your venom on Willy, I'd finally had enough of it."

Tiff stood up and was about to walk out of the room when Willy interjected, "Tiffany, I don't know how we started out on the wrong foot, but I would like to be friends. That is if you can somehow forgive us for what we're about to tell you."

Intrigued, Tiffany sat back down on the couch, crossed her arms, stared at Tommy and commanded, "Go on."

Tommy announced, "The easiest way to say this is to just come right out and tell you. There is no new hair style."

"What do you mean? I don't believe you. You showed me that picture of your mom and everything."

"That's right, but that picture of my mom is from 1986, not this summer. And as far as I know anyway, the fashion people in New York have no intention of bringing back that god-awful style. I'm sorry, but that's the truth."

Tiff had the most disbelieving look on her face, "You mean I've been walking around town telling everyone that *this* is the latest style and it's not?"

Tommy nodded her head, "That's exactly what I mean. You're just so horrible to people I thought it was time to teach you a lesson. You should know the whole idea was mine. Willy had nothing to do with it."

Tiff looked like she was about to cry. She stood up slowly and turned to Willy, "Thank you for not being a part of this. Now, would you both please leave?"

Tommy said, "Sure, but first we brought you a little something to say we're sorry."

Tiffany took the bag Tommy offered her and without saying another word walked out of the room. She left Tommy and Willy to show themselves out.

Willy said, "I don't know about you Tommy, but I feel like dirt."

"*You* feel like dirt? Imagine how I feel. It was *my* plan!"

The girls walked out of Tiffany's house feeling about an inch tall. This was one equal and opposite reaction they hoped to never have to experience again."

Chaos

Four weeks, to the day, after he left Monteith, Broadwyn (a.k.a. Broad) Beauregard Banister returned. Boxes upon boxes of supplies had started to pour into the factory over the last few weeks and had been carried to the second floor factory in anticipation of his arrival.

Mrs. C., Willy, Tommy, Charlie, Mrs. Snodgrass and Mrs. Andretti were all sitting in the front room drinking tea. They were admiring how beautiful the factory looked, now that it was all cleaned and painted. Emma Jean Snodgrass and Ginger Andretti volunteered to run the coffee bar on opening day so Willy and Tommy could walk around and model all the different wigs. That is what the ladies were discussing when everything got turned upside down.

The front door opened and in walked Broad with an astounding array of characters. They were all chatting excitedly and sounded a lot like a brood of cackling hens. Broad glided right over to Mrs. C. and declared, "Mrs. Carbunkle, you are amazing! What a lovely job you've done transforming the factory. I am more excited than I can tell you!" Then gesturing to his cohorts, added, "I would like for you to meet your new staff."

Three very unique characters lined up behind Broad and he began to introduce them. First was a woman of indeterminate years. She might have been thirty and she might have been fifty and by the way she was dressed, she might have been a man, but she wasn't. She had very, very short blonde hair and wore glasses with dark black plastic frames. Overall, she appeared to be an extremely serious person.

"Mrs. Carbunkle, ladies, this is Allysa Van Clink. Allysa is originally from Berlin, Germany. She specializes in dying and highlighting. She's a genius in her field. We are so lucky to have her."

Next a very round and balding man stepped forward. He looked surprisingly like the George character from the old television show, Seinfeld.

"This," Broad announced, "is Harvey Stingle. His specialty is making skullcaps. He is so talented that you can't even tell the caps he creates are wigs. Harvey uses an extremely lightweight mesh that forms to any head perfectly. His talent is the reason we will start receiving celebrity orders. There is no one in Hollywood that does the work as well as Harvey."

Harvey gave the ladies a slight bow and then stepped back. Then the most interesting character of them all stepped up and tilted his head to the side. The man was at least six feet five inches tall. He was very thin, about fifty or so, and wore a very elegant looking suit. He looked more like an English butler than someone who worked in a wig factory.

Broad declared, "And last, but not least, Lawrence Fenworthy. Lawrence is a man of all trades. He helps me design the wigs and he hand sews the hair into the wigs. Let's just say, there isn't much Lawrence doesn't do."

Lawrence took Mrs. C.'s hand, bent over and kissed it, and then he clicked his heels together. In a very dignified English accent, he proclaimed it was his immense pleasure to meet such a delightful array of ladies. The ladies didn't know quite what to say. By the time they got their bearings again, Broad had already hurried his staff off to the second floor to get started setting up their new work space.

Mrs. Carbunkle was the first to break the silence, "Well, if that isn't the most wonderful group of people! If they're anything like other New Yorkers, I'm sorry I've never visited. Aren't we fortunate to have such diverse new residents?"

All the ladies agreed with her that Monteith was certainly becoming interesting.

After finishing their tea, Willy and Tommy's moms started unpacking the china for the coffee bar. While that was being accomplished, Mrs. C. took the girls into the back to choose the different wigs they would wear on opening day. The idea was to have them model wigs dating back from 1889, when the factory first opened, all the way to the present. The newest wigs would be created in the next two weeks by Broad and his merry band of wig makers.

Mrs. C. also dug out old clothing that once belonged to her grandmother, mother and herself. With very slight alterations, the dresses fit the girls perfectly. It was Mrs. C.'s idea that her young friends dress according to the style of hair they were wearing. That would give the ladies of Monteith a better appreciation for the complete look each individual wig helped create.

After agreeing on several styles each, Willy and Tommy decided to take a break. They relaxed in the two styling chairs in the room behind the storeroom and were talking very animatedly about all the different costumes they got to wear when Bella, Aurelia and Athena walked in. Willy immediately informed their ghostly friends opening day was scheduled for August thirtieth.

Bella announced, "But Willy dear that just won't do! You must convince Georgie to open the shop by August the twenty-second at the very latest."

Willy gasped, "August twenty-second? How are we going to do that? That's a full week ahead of schedule and we'll just make August thirtieth if we work our tails off!"

"Girls, I'm not at liberty to tell you why the shop must be open then, but regardless, you *must* make sure it happens."

Exasperated, Tommy pleaded, "Bella, there must be something you can tell us."

"Alright Tommy, Willy, I'll tell you what I can. There is an extremely important lady that will be coming to town and she will require the services of The Willamette Wig Factory. She will be here sometime after August twenty-second, but well before August thirtieth. The shop *must* be open to help her. That is simply all I can say at this time. It's my advice you get up and get back to work. And while you're at it, you better go tell Georgie she needs to change the opening dates on her flyers before they go out."

Willy and Tommy had *no* idea how they were going to convince Mrs. C. to change the opening date. They talked about it and talked about it and then Willy came up with an idea. They would each tell their parents that they were spending the night at the other's house and then they would meet at the factory at seven o'clock. Being that their parents wouldn't expect them home until morning, they would spend the night in the old nursery on the third floor of the factory. There they would fine tune their plan.

Boy, just when they thought everything was going to work out they were thrown a curve ball. What they couldn't stop wondering though was who this important lady was and why would she need their help?

Slumber Party

Tommy and Willy met at the factory at seven o'clock as planned. They hid their bikes in the bushes by the side of the building so no one would know they were there. As soon as they got to the front door, they heard an audible click as the factory unlocked itself. Willy opened the door and the girls bolted it from inside. Then they ran up the stairs to the third floor. They unpacked their backpacks which were loaded with sodas, chips and extremely fresh cherry Twizzlers. As soon as they cracked a can of orange soda, they started talking about what to do with the fliers. After much debate, they decided they would simply change the date from August thirtieth on the prototype and type in August twenty-second. Then they would print out four hundred new fliers and distribute those around town the following morning before Mrs. C. got a chance to see them. It was a pretty horrible thing to do to their friend, but there was simply no other solution.

By eight o'clock, the girls began to wonder why they hadn't seen Bella, Aurelia or Athena. It seemed like down right bad teamwork to drop this problem in their laps and then not show up to help with a solution. They didn't waste too much time being angry though because they had a lot of work to do.

Once Willy and Tommy changed the date on the fliers, they started to make copies on the hot pink paper that Mrs. C. bought. When they'd made only fifty-six copies, they ran out of paper. Now where in the world were they going to get three-hundred-and-forty-four more sheets of hot pink paper at that hour? After all their planning, they had hit a brick wall. Tommy declared, "That's it Willy, I give up. I mean this is just too big of a problem for us to solve all by ourselves."

Just as Willy agreed giving up was the way to go, three hundred and forty-four sheets of hot pink paper fell out of the ceiling on them. The friends laughed their heads off in surprise and relief. That was the confirmation they needed that their idea had met with the approval of their other-worldly conspirators. The girls gathered the paper as fast as possible and ran off the rest of their copies. Then they divided them for early distribution the following morning. They each stuck half a stack into their respective backpacks and started to seriously think about going to sleep. They were exhausted from all the work they had been doing recently.

Once the girls had curled up on the two Victorian couches on the third floor and were just about to doze off, they heard what sounded like a waltz. The music seemed to be coming from the downstairs. Willy grumbled, "Oh for crying out loud. You would think they would want us to get our sleep so we can get to work at the crack of dawn. After all, that's the only way we'll ever be ready to open by the twenty-second."

Tommy added, "We better go down and see what they want."

The friends got up, put their slippers on and started to walk down the stairs. They were talking to each other on the way when they heard a man's voice. It sounded like Lawrence Fenworthy of all people. What was he doing here at this time of night? The girls got very quiet and started to tip toe down the remaining stairs to investigate. By the time they reached the first floor, they heard a woman laugh. Holy bats, he was with a woman! What was going on? The sound of voices and music seemed to be coming from The Annex. The girls crept like mice towards the back room. After all, it wouldn't do to get caught and then have to explain what *they* were doing in the factory at that time of night, in their pajamas of all things.

What Willy and Tommy saw when they looked into The Annex caused them to jump in surprise. Mr. Fenworthy was all decked out in a tuxedo. He must have lit a million candles and he was dancing with the most beautiful lady either girl had ever seen. The lady was wearing a long white gown that clung to her body like a second skin. It had a flippy little train at the end that fluttered every time Mr. Fenworthy spun her around.

The mystery woman had auburn hair, the same color as the freshly polished copper pans that hung in Tommy's kitchen. She was absolutely stunning! She also had a very throaty kind of laugh and she almost purred in her strong German accent, "Larry darlink, you are soooooo graceful. I luf dancing vit you more dan anytink else in da vorld!"

Willy and Tommy almost fell over because the gorgeous woman dancing with "Larry" was none other than Allysa Van Clink. Unbelievable. Holy moly, what power a wig had! Willy would wear wigs everyday if she could look like that. Neither girl knew what to do next, so they watched Mr. Fenworthy and Miss Van Clink dance for another hour. They were so graceful and beautiful. Both girls fantasized about what it would be like to glide around a room drenched in candle light, in the arms of a handsome boy. They were so caught up in the romance they didn't realize when the music ended until Mr. Fenworthy and Miss Van Clink started to leave the room. They managed to slide into the storeroom in the nick of time to avoid detection.

After the dancers left the factory, Tommy and Willy went back up to the third floor. They couldn't fall sleep as they were so curious over the interesting new development they just witnessed. Tommy declared, "You know, I actually like them better after seeing them tonight. They didn't seem very human before did they? And now, they're just so, so, romantic."

Willy agreed, "I know what you mean. Miss Van Clink was positively scary this afternoon. Who would have thought she was such a babe? Too bad we can't tell anyone what we saw."

The friends continued to chat and it wasn't until after one a.m. when they finally drifted off to sleep. It was a good thing Willy thought to bring an alarm clock, because there was no way they could have wakened at six o'clock on their own. When the alarm went off, neither girl wanted to wake up to turn it off. Finally, the ringing stopped, but only because it was driving Bella nuts and *she* turned it off.

"Girls, get up!" she admonished. "This is what

you get for spying all night. Move, move, move...
Let's go, you have a job to do!"

Amidst a lot of groaning, grumbling, and complaining about how unfair life was, Tommy and Willy dragged themselves from sleep and got dressed. Ten minutes later, they left the factory, grabbed their bikes and started distributing the fliers around town. It took them three hours to get them safely tucked into all the mailboxes. After they were done, they stopped by The Plucky Pig to order a huge stack of hotcakes for breakfast. They lingered as long as they could because they knew when they got back to the factory, it was all going to hit the fan.

Recovery

Sitting in The Plucky Pig, over Mr. Jim's Mancakes, Tommy suddenly became very alarmed. "Willy, what would be the worst mistake that we could have made last night?"

"Mistake, what do you mean? We were brilliant."

"Will, think a minute. What were we about to do when we heard that music?"

"What do you mean? We were about to go to sleep."

Tommy was getting frustrated. "Yeah, but what were we going to do right before going to sleep?"

"Oh my gosh…oh no…you mean…oh man…we were going to put the old fliers into a bag so we wouldn't forget to throw them into the dumpster this morning. Tommy, please tell me you did that, please!"

Tommy sarcastically asked, "Hmmm, when would I have done that, do you think? I was with you the whole time."

In a panic, the girls threw money on the table, probably leaving Mr. Jim a sixty percent tip because there was no way they could wait for change. As they flew down First Street on their bikes, Tommy screamed, "You go to the factory and destroy the evidence. I'm going to go to Mrs. Carbunkle's house and try to stall her."

Willy couldn't remember ever getting someplace so fast in her whole life. She dropped her bike in front of the factory, waited till she heard the click of the lock and ran up three flights of stairs. She figured, it took her about six seconds. When she reached the third floor the first thing she saw was Mrs. Carbunkle. Mrs. C. was sitting on the couch sipping a cup of tea.

"Wilhelmina dear, where have you been? We've got so much work to do. Where is Thomasina?"

"Tommy is uh… she's ummm…I mean she's…on her way."

"Are you feeling well dear? If not, I suppose you could distribute the fliers tomorrow."

"The fliers? Have you seen the fliers?"

Mrs. C. answered, "No dear, I haven't but I'm sure they're here somewhere."

Willy announced, "Well, Mrs. C., the reason you haven't seen them is because Tommy and I delivered them this morning. That's why Tommy isn't here yet. She's finishing up."

Delighted, Mrs. C. exclaimed, "You're fooling! That's wonderful news! You girls are so industrious. I don't know how I could have done this all without you." While Mrs. C. was talking, Willy was covertly looking all over the room trying to locate the old stack of fliers. She couldn't find them anywhere. She started to panic just as she felt a note get slipped into her hand. She figured it was probably from Bella. The note said:

Willy Dear,

That was a little too close for comfort, don't you think? You will find what you are looking for in the ladies' room on the first floor. Walk in, lock the door, and don't dilly dally.

Fondly,
Aunt Bella

Willy mumbled something to Mrs. C. about needing to check on something and then ran downstairs to the bathroom. As soon as she got there, she made sure she was alone and then she locked the door. As soon as the bolt slipped into place, she felt a breeze start to flow through the room. She noticed that the window was closed just as four-hundred sheets of hot pink paper blew in. The whole room was covered in old fliers. Willy shouted above the fluttering paper, "Am I wrong or is this a little dramatic? Geez, did it ever occur to you guys to leave them in a stack on the sink or something?"

Willy was on her hands and knees collecting all the fliers when she could have sworn she heard laughter. She shook her head and smiled. She decided that she had just been taught another lesson. Something along the lines of, "Take the time to make sure it's done right the first time." She realized she should just be grateful that Bella, Aurelia and Athena had come to their rescue.

Discovery

There was no way around it. Willy and Tommy knew they were about to be found out. The moment of truth came when Mrs. C. asked the girls for a copy of the flier so she could tape it to the front door of the factory. Willy offered to do it for her, but Mrs. C. said that she wanted to do it all by herself. After all, since she was the one who closed up shop, she wanted to be the one to post the notice about it reopening. There was no arguing with that. Willy got Mrs. C. a flier and tape and then handed it to her.

Mrs. C. scanned the flier and inquired, "What's this? This isn't what I wrote. Did you girls change it?"

The friends were shaking in their boots now. Tommy innocently asked, "What do you mean, Mrs. C.? That's the flier you left for us so that's the flier we distributed. What's wrong with it?" Playing dumb was their only hope.

Mrs. C. said, "Look here girls, I wrote, Georgianna Carbunkle invites you to the grand reopening of "The Willamette Wig Factory." Now see what the flier says."

The flier even surprised Willy and Tommy. It read:

Bella Barnes-Bennet, Aurelia Bennet-Cox,
Athena Cox-Barlett
& Georgianna Barlett-Carbunkle

Invite all the lovely women
of the Willamette Valley

to join us in CELEBRATING the
reopening of

The Willamette Wig Factory

There will be refreshments & informal
modeling.

58 Walnut Alley
Monteith, Oregon

We will expect you between 10 a.m. & 5 p.m.
Saturday, August 22nd

Come and discover that change doesn't
need to be permanent.

Mrs. C. asked, "Girls, are you sure you didn't rewrite this? I mean, it is just wonderful! To think that it never occurred to me to use my dear relatives' names in the invitation. How very thoughtless of me. After all, if it weren't for them, the factory wouldn't exist. It's just so lovely."

Willy and Tommy were totally perplexed. How did this happen? Obviously, Bella, Aurelia and Athena had been behind it. The question was how had they not noticed? After all, they had just delivered four hundred of them. They were still trying to piece it together when they heard Mrs. C. yell out, "August twenty-second?! WHAT?! How can we be open August twenty-second? Oh my goodness, oh my heavens, sweet Lord above! Girls, quit standing there and go get young Broadwyn. We must tell him the date has moved. Hurry… Run… GOOOOOOO!!!"

How about that? In all the excitement over the changed flier, Mrs. Carbunkle wasn't even going to question the opening date. That was wonderful news. Now all Willy and Tommy had to do was to work like the very dickens and perhaps give up sleep because The Willamette Wig Factory would be opening in only six days.

Mrs. Carbunkle spoke with Broadwyn and promised a healthy bonus for his entire staff if they could make enough wigs to have the factory ready in time. Broad was a little alarmed by the change, but like a trouper he declared, "Mrs. Carbunkle, we are professionals. We will be ready. Now if you will excuse me, I have a considerable amount of work ahead of me." Broad was still talking as he backed out of the room. The girls could hear him issuing orders to his staff. It sounded more like twenty people were working on the second floor rather than just four.

Willy, Tommy, and Mrs. C. all went to The Annex to finish choosing the wigs and costumes they would be wearing on opening day. Once they were done, the girls took all the dresses to the dry cleaner to freshen them up. Then they went right back to the factory to polish silver forks for the coffee room. Once they were done polishing, they ironed and folded the napkins Mrs. C. bought. This was going to be a long day so they decided to order pizzas for lunch. Everyone would simply be too busy to feed themselves. Because in only six days the factory would be open for business!

Chameleon

The town of Monteith was very excited about the reopening of the wig factory. Most of the women who would be attending didn't even remember when the original factory was open. A lot of them hadn't even lived in Monteith then and some hadn't even been born. Quite simply, the majority of women didn't even wear wigs anymore. Yet there was still a feverish quality in the air. People were acting like the circus was coming to town. Betty Lou, at The House of Style, was heard saying that she hadn't sold so many new dresses in a week's time in the entire forty-eight year history of her store.

The House of Style was the one dress shop in Monteith that catered to the high-end fashion conscious residents of town. The clothes very pricey but they were classy and well-made. Legend had it that a certain lady from Los Angeles had been visiting her aunt in Monteith when her husband called in a panic. He told her, "Honey, get on the first plane to London. The meeting that got cancelled is back on. Buy all new clothes in Oregon because you don't have time to come home and pack. I'm already on my way to the airport!" The lady was furious with her husband. Buy all new clothes in Monteith? She doubted there were any clothes in all of the stores in all of the Willamette Valley that would even be appropriate to wear to bed in London, let alone outfit her for grand functions. Was he mad? That was when her aunt told her about The House of Style. The woman spent a reported five thousand dollars there in one afternoon, which was more than Betty Lou normally sold in two months. The lady's name was Mrs. Austin Smythe-Greggor and she wrote a lovely letter to Betty Lou when she returned to Los Angeles. In her note, she said that she wore the black organza evening dress to be presented to the Queen who went on to compliment her exquisite dress. That is the kind of establishment Betty Lou ran. So for her to be selling the number of dresses she had, for the opening of a wig factory, you better believe Monteith was excited.

Ginger Andretti went to buy a new dress as well. When she heard about the rush on Betty Lou's merchandise she had an idea. As soon as she found what she was looking for, Ginger went right over to the wig factory to talk with Mrs. C. Once she had a steaming hot cup of morning jasmine tea in front of her, she disclosed her plan. Mrs. C. loved the idea. It was just the right extra touch to offer a few lucky gals in town.

Ginger's plan was to hold a raffle. The ladies at the door would all be given a numbered ticket when they walked in. At ten-thirty, three names would be drawn and those three lucky ladies would be swept away to the third floor for an exciting make over. Mrs. C. would give them each a wig of their choice and Ginger would apply their make-up. When they were done, they would join the rest of the ladies on the first floor. This way the ladies of the Willamette Valley could see first-hand what an amazing transformation a wig could make. Once Betty Lou heard about the plan, she jumped on board. She told Ginger she would come over right at ten-thirty to see who the winners were. Then she would go back to her shop and choose a dress for each of them. It would be her way of showing Mrs. Carbunkle how appreciative she was for all the extra business the opening brought her store.

Mrs. C. told Willy and Tommy about the idea and they were very excited. They, themselves, would be having continuous makeovers during the day, what with their extensive modeling duties. Willy got to thinking if only the women could see a before and after of Allysa Van Clink, there wouldn't be a wig left in the whole factory. She needed to talk to Allysa right away.

When Willy found Allysa, she didn't really know how to go about talking to her. She wound up shadowing her for about ten minutes before jumping in with, "Hi Miss Van Clink. Are you busy?"

The stern German colorist replied, "Oh my, ja. Vee are extremely busy. Vat do you vant?"

"Well, Tommy and I are going to be modeling the wigs on Saturday and Mrs. C. will be wearing one. I just thought maybe you might wear one too. You know, to help show the ladies of the Willamette Valley all the styles available."

"I do not like to vear vigs, Meess Snodgrass. I do not enjoy people looking at me."

Willy couldn't believe what she was hearing. Miss Van Clink was gorgeous when she wore a wig and girlie clothes. Why wouldn't she want people to see her like that? She conceded, "Okay. I just thought because you're so beautiful and all, you might want to help. But you don't have to."

Perplexed, Allysa responded, "Yoo sink I am beautiful? Vhy vould you sink zat? It ees not true. Look at my glasses, look at my hair. Zeese are not beautiful."

"Your glasses and hair aren't *you*. You could take the glasses off, wear a wig and maybe put on a dress. I bet there wouldn't be anyone who could equal you. Even Tommy's mom and she was a model."

Allysa softened slightly, "I vill sink about eet, ja? But no guarantees."

Willy was delighted. She didn't know if Miss Van Clink would do it or not, but she was going to hope like crazy she would. On her way down the stairs, Willy passed Mr. Fenworthy. Lawrence had overheard everything Willy said to Allysa. He went over to Allyssa, put his arm around her shoulder and said, "I think you should do it Allysa. I think you should show these people what a glamorous woman you are."

Allysa blushed and smiled. She clearly enjoyed the praise from Lawrence. She told him she would think about it.

Backfire

In all the hoopla over reopening the wig factory, Willy barely noticed that Jamie Armstrong hadn't been to church the last few weeks. She asked Tommy about it and Tommy told her he went off to basketball camp for a month. So, when Willy was walking down First Street to pick up the dresses for the opening, she was delighted to see Jamie walking toward her. Wow, this whole summer was turning out just great! Jamie smiled when he saw Willy. He even offered to carry the dry cleaning back to the factory. Then he asked her how her summer was going. She told him all about the factory and finding out how she was related to Mrs. C. Willy asked Jamie how *his* summer was going. He told her about basketball camp and how he was mowing lawns in his neighborhood for extra money.

About a block before they got to the factory, Jamie asked Willy if she had any other run-ins with

Tiffany. Willy stumbled on a crack in the sidewalk and wondered what she should tell him. Had he heard about the hair incident? She didn't know what to say, so she decided to be evasive.

"Oh, I've seen her around at The Plucky Pig and stuff like that. I'm not sure we're going to be great friends or anything. Although, I don't think she actively hates me anymore. So that's good news."

Jamie admitted, "Actually, you're right about that. The day after I got home from camp, she stopped by my house. We had a really nice talk and she told me all about the hair prank Tommy played on her. She also told me you didn't have anything to do with it. She really appreciated your apology." Then he added, "By the way, tell Tommy I thought it was hysterical. Tiff showed me what it looked like under her wig and I had a hard time not laughing."

Willy was confused. What was going on here? Tiffany went over to Jamie's house? She showed him her hair? Why? What else did they talk about? This was not good. As all of these things were running through her head Jamie continued, "Anyway, I think Tiff really learned her lesson. She said she felt really bad about the way she treated you and she also told me she felt bad about some stuff she did last year. So thanks, I don't think Tiff and I would be going out again without you guys."

When they arrived at the factory, Jamie handed Willy the dresses. She just stood there with her mouth open like she was trying to catch flies. What just happened? The nasty diva Tiffany got the guy? How, how, how?! And it wouldn't have happened without *her*? She thought she was going to be sick. Jamie just smiled and said, "Anyway, I better let you go. It sounds like you've got tons of work to do and I promised to be at Tiff's five minutes ago. See you Saturday, okay?"

"Saturday?"

"Yeah, I'm coming to the opening with Tiff and her mom. I know it's kind of girlie, but I promised I'd help her pick out another wig."

Willy stammered, "Uhhhh... oohhhhh... well... ummmm... I'll see you Saturday then. Bye." As soon as Jamie walked away, Will stamped her foot and let out a rather loud sound of protest.

As she was about to walk back into the factory, she noticed Bobby was on the carousel again. He waved and called out, "Problems?"

Willy stormed over to the fence and demanded, "What is wrong with you boys? Why do you always go for the superficial girls?"

Bobby laughed, "Ah, boy trouble, huh? Not sure I'm the guy with answers for you though."

"Why, are you the only normal guy left in the

world?"

Bobby smiled, "Hey, looks like you're doing wonders with the old wig factory. Nice work. Any chance you want to take on the carousel when you're done?"

Willy shook her head, "Are you kidding me? Tommy and I are going to be so busy with school and the factory we'd never have the time. Why don't you take it on?"

Bobby answered, "I'm trying to, but it seems to be a little more than I can handle on my own."

"I'll talk to Tommy about it. Maybe she has some ideas."

Her new friend replied, "That would be great, thanks!" Then he picked up his book and added, "I better get going. I want to go hang out with my mom for a while."

Willy thought that was really sweet. Bobby was a nice kid. Too bad he didn't live in Monteith anymore.

When Willy got back to the factory, she started to brood about Jamie and Tiff again. Something this bad could only happen to her and she owed it all to her new best friend. She was so mad she could spit! Willy walked into the front room and immediately saw her friend. Tommy noticed the murderous look right away and turned to make a run for the restroom. That's when Willy realized Tommy must already know about Jamie and Tiff. Why hadn't she shared the information? Willy ran after Tommy and slammed into the ladies' room just in time to hear her friend lock herself into a stall.

Tommy called out, "Willy, before you say anything, I am sooooo sorry. I know you like Jamie and had hopes for the two of you. I mean, who would have guessed he would ever go back with Tiff? I know it's all my fault. I mean if I didn't wreck her hair, she wouldn't have realized people don't like her and she never would have apologized to him. I am just so so so so so so so so so so so so so sorry. Do you forgive me?"

Willy realized then the whole situation was totally funny. Not in a million years could Tommy have ever known what would happen and the only reason she played that trick on Tiff was to get even for what Tiff said about her. There was also the factory to consider. Seeing Tiffany's hair was the final straw for Mrs. C. It was that horrific cut that propelled Mrs. C. into action to reopen the factory. Willy couldn't help it. She started to giggle and once she started, she couldn't stop. She sat on the chaise and laughed until tears streamed down her face. She could hear Tommy in the background asking, "Willy, are you okay? Willy? Is this a trick to get me to come out?"

Tommy crept out from the safety of the stall and saw her friend. The laughter turned infectious. She started to chuckle too. Then she made eye contact with Willy and the two of them fell completely apart. Neither one of them saw Bella, Aurelia and Athena standing in the corner nor did they hear Bella say, "My goodness, I'm delighted that turned out for the best. Whatever was Jamie Armstrong thinking?"

The Best Day Ever

Saturday, August twenty-second, turned out to be the best day ever in the life of Wilhelmina Rhonda Snodgrass. She and Tommy both stayed at their own houses the night before so they could get a really, good night's rest. They knew if they spent the night together, they wouldn't sleep a wink. They would have been too busy talking about the next day's events. Mrs. Carbunkle asked her staff and helpers to please meet her at the factory at eight-thirty for a special celebration breakfast. Willy and her mom hopped in their station wagon at ten after eight and by the time they found parking and got all their stuff unloaded, they walked through the door of the factory at eight-thirty sharp. Tommy, Charlie, and their mom were already there. Broad, Harvey, Lawrence, and Allysa were on the second floor doing last minute touch-ups and Mrs. C. was in the kitchen wearing a bright yellow apron, singing Morning Has

Broken, at the top of her lungs. It was a perfect morning. Everyone sat down together in the kitchen to eat and discuss the itinerary for the day. Mrs. C. was the hostess, so she would walk around and talk to all of the guests. Willy's mom was going to run the coffee bar with help from Charlie. Mrs. Andretti would be upstairs making over three lucky town's ladies. Willy and Charlie would be walking all over the factory modeling their wigs and Broadwyn, Harvey, Lawrence, and Allysa were going to work The Annex. They would answer questions, ring up sales and make appointments for custom fittings. Mrs. C. asked if anyone could think of anything else. Everyone thought that about covered it, so they hurriedly finished up so they could get back to work.

Mrs. C. asked Willy and Tommy to please stay a moment. She exclaimed, "Dears, I just want to tell you what your wonderful friendship has meant to me. I couldn't and wouldn't have done any of this without you. Now, if you will both come over here and give an old lady a hug and kiss, I have a favor to ask of you."

Both girls ran to Mrs. C. and wrapped their arms around her. They didn't think their old friend would ever know what this summer had meant to them, either. So when they hugged her, they tried to convey all of their emotions in that embrace.

Mrs. C. pulled away from them and said, "Sit down girls. First of all, I have an envelope for each of you. Please take these and put them in a safe place. Secondly, I don't want either of you to call me Mrs. C. anymore. I'm wondering if you would do me the honor of calling me Aunt Georgianna. What do you think?"

Tommy was the first to answer, "No can do Mrs. C. I gotta tell you, 'Aunt Georgianna' feels like I'm trying to talk with a mouth full of marbles. I can call you Mrs. C. or Aunt George. You pick."

Mrs. C. declared, "Aunt George? That sounds like I'm your uncle in a dress. I don't know what I think about that. What do you think, Wilhelmina?"

"I think I'd like to call you Aunt Georgie. How does that sound?"

Mrs. C.'s eyes filled up with tears and she said she thought that sounded just fine. She told the girls how her mother, grandmother, and great grandmother had called her Georgie and she loved it. Having the girls call her that would be like having her family back.

Bella, Aurelia and Athena were standing in the corner witnessing this very touching scene. They were so glad they were given the opportunity to come back and help their Georgie. It was wonderful to see her hugging the next generation of the family right there in the factory. Even though Tommy wasn't technically a blood relation, they considered her one after all her wonderful work. And Willy, dear Willy, meant the factory just might carry on for many more generations to come.

Aunt Georgie gave the girls one last big squeeze and told them they better run off and get their make-up done and get into their first costume. The girls virtually floated up the stairs. When they got there, they ripped open their envelopes and found bankbooks. They were a little puzzled. Willy opened hers up and the names on the first page said, Wilhelmina Rhonda Snodgrass/Georgianna Carbunkle. The balance in the book read $1000.00! Holy cow, what was this all about? Tommy's pass book said, Thomasina Franchesca Andretti/Georgianna Carbunkle, with the same balance. The girls just stared at each other. That's when a note fell out of Willy's passbook. It read:

Wilhelmina Dear,

You have brought quite a lot of excitement to my old life and I don't know how to begin to repay you. The passbook is not repayment for your friendship. It is merely an estimate of what I owe you for all your hard work to date. The passbook is primarily a savings account. I will be paying you $7.00/ hour *from now on, when you work at the factory. Half of your wages must be deposited in the bank. The other half, you may spend as you see fit. My name is on your account as well, as I will be checking up on you, dear. You will not be able to withdraw money without my signature until you are eighteen. This is not because I don't trust you. It is simply because I was almost twelve once myself and know what great temptations lie in store. Now quit reading this note and get dressed.*

> *All My Love,*
> *Aunt Georgianna*

Tommy had a very similar letter with one addition. Aunt Georgie wrote:

Thomasina, now that the factory is reopening, I find myself much less concerned over the oddities you perform with your hair. Now, if you ever do something irreparable, we will have a multitude of ways to fix it.

Tommy had to smile because she knew that as much as Aunt Georgie carried on about her hair, she secretly liked it.

Willy and Tommy stashed their passbooks in their backpacks and started to get ready for the day. First,

Mrs. Andretti did their make-up, then they put on their first costume, and finally, they went to the second floor where Broadwyn had all their wigs lined up. They were on numbered heads corresponding with the numbers pinned to the dresses upstairs. This way, they wouldn't accidentally wind up wearing an outfit from the fifties with a hairstyle from the twenties. It was a great safety net Broad himself came up with.

The girls ran downstairs to see how everyone else was getting along and almost knocked over a photographer. The Montieth Valley Biweekly Bee had come to take a photo for Thursday's addition. They asked Aunt Georgie to stand in The Annex so they could photograph her in front of the older wigs. She said she would do one photo like that but only if they used a larger photo of her entire staff. After all, without them, the factory would have never reopened. The photographer loved the idea once he saw the odd array of participants. He arranged everyone into three rows with the tallest in back and the shortest in front. Willy, Aunt Georgie and Tommy were the front row. Just as the photo snapped, Bella, Aurelia and Athena situated themselves in a brand new fourth row, right behind Aunt Georgie and the girls. It was a beautiful picture. The townspeople marveled at what a wonderful job the photographer did superimposing the three women from the past into the scene. However, when the photographer saw the picture, he decided he needed a vacation. The day after the Thursday edition came out he left for an extended trip to Hawaii.

Grand Opening

No one really knew what kind of crowd to expect when the doors opened. The flier said the opening was from ten to five. But this was Monteith, a town without that many grand functions. Being the women bought new dresses for the event, you can believe no one was going to show up even one minute after ten. They wanted the full seven hours in which to shop, socialize and check out the new factory. They weren't going to miss a second of it.

Mrs. Snodgrass and Charlie set several trays of cookies along the counter of the coffee bar. Being that today was the grand opening all of the refreshments were complimentary. They also set up two beverage tables. One served coffee, the other, Lady Blush Punch.

Aunt Georgie entered the front room wearing a Gibson Girl wig and a long empire-waist styled dress. She looked lovely. Emma Jean Snodgrass wore a wig from the 1950's that made her look remarkably like Marilyn Monroe. She complimented it with a very full-skirted sundress. Charlie decided to represent the punk eighties and wore her mom's hot pink, spiked wig from that same era. For their first outfits, both Willy and Tommy wore dresses from the 1880's.

Just when they were about to open the door, Allysa Van Clink descended the staircase. Everyone stared in awe. Allysa wore a very slinky silver gown from the 1940's that had a low-neckline with the entire back plunging almost to her bottom. The skirt was tight to her thighs and then pooled down to the floor. Like the dress she wore that night with Lawrence Fenworthy, this one also had a small train. Her wig looked like a movie star's. It was platinum blonde and went just past her shoulders. It was parted on the side and crimped away from her face. The whole effect was so stunning they all stared at her for what felt like an eternity. Lawrence walked forward and offered her his arm. That is when everyone started to applaud. Allysa was extremely embarrassed and very pleased by the attention.

Now with everyone assembled, it was time to open the doors. Aunt Georgie slid the dead bolt, opened the door wide and let in what seemed like a thousand ladies and girls from Monteith and neighboring towns. She quickly stepped aside lest she get trampled and made her way to The Annex to mingle. Charlie handed out tickets for the door prizes and Mrs. Snodgrass handed out cups of punch. At exactly ten-thirty, Aunt Georgie went to the microphone and quieted the crowd. She proceeded to tell them what the prize was if their raffle number was called. The ladies glazed over in excitement. Which one of them wouldn't want a complete makeover? Aunt Georgie called the first number, which happily turned out to be Miss Bickle from The Clothes Horse. That secretly thrilled Georgianna because in all honesty, no one could use a make-over more. The second number was called and lo and behold it was none other than Belinda Smoot, from the pharmacy. This was just getting better and better. The third makeover went to Bernadette Clump. Bernie was the wife of a pig farmer. They lived on the outskirts of town and if you asked anyone in the Willamette Valley, they would tell you they thought that as well as making all her own clothes, Bernadette also cut her own hair. No one deserved a new dress and transformation more than she did.

Ginger clucked and fussed over the ladies and ushered them to the third floor to begin their metamorphosis. When she got them upstairs, she had them all put on fluffy, white terry cloth robes. Charlie brought them steaming cups of coffee and cranberry scones, just like they were in a real fancy salon. True to her word, Betty Lou from The House of Style showed up to assess the winners for new dresses. They conferred as to which wig each of the ladies was going to receive in order to give Betty Lou an idea what dress she would choose for them. The winners sat on the sofa and talked excitedly about the day ahead of them. The whole third floor was devoid of mirrors so the winners couldn't see what was transpiring. Ginger started working on the makeup and the third floor became a hive of activity.

Meanwhile, downstairs in The Annex, the town's women began trying on wigs. Bella, Aurelia and Athena were circulating among them. Of course, no one other than Willy or Tommy actually saw them. Bella was helping the women decide which wig would suit them best. LaVaonda Tremaine, from Diabolical Cleaners, seemed to have her own ideas though. She picked up one bad choice after another. Whenever she put on a wig that didn't look good on her, Bella pushed it off her head. LaVonda was heard telling a friend there was something wrong with these wigs. At that point her friend chose one for her that Bella had been trying to get on LaVonda's head all morning. LaVonda said she thought that particular style was all wrong for her but at her friend's urging she tried it on anyway. LaVonda barely glanced at herself in the mirror before she started to pull the wig off. That was when Bella plopped her hand right on top of LaVonda's head and refused to let her take it off until she got a good look at herself. Tommy chose that moment to go over and tell Mrs. Tremaine how amazing she looked. That's when LaVonda really looked at herself. She pulled out her checkbook and bought one in blonde, auburn, and dark brown!

Willy and Tommy were laughing at Bella's machinations when they noticed Bobby walk in. Tommy called out, "Hey Bobby, fancy meeting you here."

Bobby hurried over to his new friends, "Hey, yourselves. You girls did a fabulous job with this old place!"

Willy replied, "Thanks, but what are you doing here?"

"Oh, I just came in looking for my mom." Then looked across the room and pointed, "There she is."

Willy and Tommy looked but they didn't see Bobby's mom. They saw a lady with graying blonde hair and bifocals who looked like she was about seventy. Tommy asked, "Where is she? I don't see her."

Bobby pointed again, "Right there."

Looking confused, Willy asked, "Is that your grandma?"

"Nope. That's my mom."

Tommy interjected, "Um, Bobby. That can't be your mom, she's too old."

At that moment Bella walked over and joined them. Bobby looked up and smiled, "Hey Bella, congratulations on the reopening!"

Willy and Tommy were astounded that Bobby could see Bella when even Aunt Georgie couldn't see her and she was family. Bella smiled, "Thanks for coming, Bobby. Did you see your mom over by the case from the 1960's?"

Bobby answered, "I sure did. She looks pretty today, doesn't she?"

Tommy interrupted, "Excuse me, but what's going on here?" To Bella, she asked, "How in the world do you know Bobby?" and to Bobby she asked, "How can you see Bella? We're the only ones who can see her."

Bella answered for both of them. "Bobby is a friend of ours. We often see him sitting on the carousel when we come to visit the factory."

Willy turned her attention to Bobby and exclaimed, "Wait a second. Bobby, are you a ghost too?"

Shrugging his shoulders, Bobby answered, "I'm like Bella, Aurelia and Athena. Not so much a ghost as an angel." He explained, "While Bella and the girls' mission was to get the factory reopened, I'm here to get the carousel rebuilt."

Completely stunned, Tommy said, "I have at least a million questions but I don't know where to start." Taking a deep breath she asked, "How old were you when you died? How did you die? Why do you want the carousel rebuilt?"

Before she could fire out any more questions, Bobby answered, "I died the month before I turned twelve. I fell out of the loft in our barn. That was almost forty years ago."

Willy and Tommy's eyes immediately filled with tears. They couldn't imagine anything so horrible. He added. "I want the carousel rebuilt because it was a huge dream my mom and I shared. I know if I can get it up and running, she would visit it all the time and have wonderful memories of our life together."

Willy cried, "Oh my gosh, that is the sweetest and saddest thing I've ever heard. How can we help?"

Bella answered for Bobby, "Once the factory is up and running, we would like you girls to help campaign to bring the carousel back. Monteith will be a buzz with excitement over the wig factory reopening and will be ripe for a new project."

Tommy exhaled, "Amazing. This is all so amazing. I don't know what to say, except that of course we'll help."

Willy agreed, "You bet we will. Just let us know what to do, Bobby, and we're in."

Bobby thanked his new friends and Bella, "I'll talk to you more about my plans soon. But now I want to go over and hang out with my mom for a while."

Willy, Tommy and Bella watched as Bobby joined his mother. She didn't see him but he put his arm around her and gave her a hug anyway.

Not So Reformed After All

Willy was so preoccupied thinking about Bobby and his mom she didn't even think about Jamie Armstrong until she saw him walking towards her. Her heart started to beat in double-time and she had to remind herself Jamie was going out with Tiff. Jamie came up to her and told her how great she looked and said he was having a surprisingly good time.

He told her he had been playing with a funny little white dog out front for the last hour. "A little white dog?" Willy asked if he knew the dog's name and Jamie said he was wearing a collar that said "Jingle" on it. Jingle? How could Jamie Armstrong see a ghost dog? At least she knew Jamie wasn't a ghost, thank goodness. But she was feeling more and more depressed. How could Jamie be dating Tiff, when he was able to see *her* family's ghost dog? Jamie told her to keep up the good work. He said he promised to get Tiff some punch and he would talk to her later.

Just as Jamie walked away, Tiffany joined her. Willy tried to smile, knowing she had already been taught a pretty tough lesson. Tiffany smiled too, but hers was more like a sneer.

Willy asked, "Hey Tiffany, are you having fun?"

This was the first time she saw Tiff since the day she and Tommy apologized and gave her the wig. Tiff was wearing the wig and it looked as natural as her own hair.

The cheerleader gloated, "Yes, I'm having fun. You may have heard Jamie and I are dating again."

Willy saw Jamie coming up behind Tiff with her punch and answered, "Yeah, I did. Congratulations, he's a really great guy."

Jamie was about to tell Tiffany he was there, when he heard her threaten, "So *Willy*, I thought you better know that Jamie Armstrong is mine and you are to stay away from him. I don't want to even hear that you've spoken to him. I don't want you to look at him. I don't even want you to *think* about him. Am I making myself clear?"

Willy responded, "Perfectly."

"Good, because even though Tommy says you had nothing to do with ruining my hair, I don't believe her. I think you're a trashy, common, conniving, piece of dirt and I'm sure it was all your idea. Please remember I can make your life at Monteith Junior High a complete nightmare and I plan on doing just that."

Jamie stood behind Tiff with his mouth wide open in shock. He thought she had changed. He thought she was sorry. Wow, was he under the wrong impression.

Willy asked, "Is there anything else, Tiff?"

"Not for the moment. Just stay out of my way."

As Tiffany turned to storm away, she ran right into Jamie and wound up wearing her cup of Lady Blush Punch. She stammered, "Oh, my goodness, Jamie. Did you just get here?"

"No Tiff, I've been here for awhile."

Tiffany said, "Did you hear all those horrible things Willy said to me? Like how she was going to try to steal you away from me?"

"No Tiff, I didn't hear anything like that."

"She must have said it before you walked up then."

"Actually Tiff, she didn't. I was only about five steps behind you. I would have

heard if she said that to you."

Tiffany realized she lost and the only way she could save face was to say, "Jamie, I've been thinking that maybe we shouldn't go out again after all. I mean, I just don't think you're my type."

Jamie answered, "I think you're absolutely right, Tiff. I'm not your type at all."

With that, Jamie asked Willy if she wanted to get some cookies with him. They walked off leaving Tiff standing in the middle of The Annex all by herself, covered in pink punch.

Finale

At two p.m. Ginger Andretti went to the microphone to announce that the winners of the door prizes had undergone their transformations and were now ready to be presented. The photographer from the Bi-Weekly Bee set up his equipment right in front of Ginger so when the winners walked out, he could snap their picture for the newspaper. He had taken their before shots earlier in the morning on the third floor.

Ginger announced, "First ladies, I have to tell you how much fun I've had today. I've talked with Mrs. Carbunkle and we've decided I will come to the factory one day a week and provide a make-over service for any lady purchasing a custom-made design. If you'd like to order a custom-made wig, please see Broadwyn Banister. He is the factory's designer."

Ginger motioned to Broad, who took a bow for

the ladies.

She continued, "Now, without further ado, I give you, Elsie Bickle, from Monteith's very own Clothes Horse."

Miss Bickle cautiously walked out from behind the curtained off area at the side of the room. The crowd went completely silent. You could have heard a hair pin drop. This was not the mousy, Miss Bickle they'd known all these years. This was a princess! Miss Bickle was wearing a black linen sheath dress that hit six inches below the knee. She had on black and white spectator pumps and gone was the mousy brown hair. She sported a silky straight auburn wig (with honey highlights) blunt cut at her shoulders. Her make-up was done in all warm golden tones and she had on 24K coral lipstick. The crowd went wild! Ginger interrupted them after about five minutes and said, "Thank you, Miss Bickle."

Elsie, who had never stood in front of a crowd before in her life, just smiled and curtseyed and waved. She showed no interest in leaving. It wasn't until Ginger started the next introduction that she reluctantly stepped back behind the curtain.

"Now ladies, I give you, Belinda Smoot!"

Belinda stepped forward and instead of being silent, the crowd immediately started clapping and cheering. Belinda, with the unfortunate frosted hair, strutted out like she was Miss America. She wasn't a day younger than fifty and she worked it like an eighteen-year old prom queen. She wiggled and sashayed and blew kisses. She was having the time of her life. She now had dark blonde, curly hair that was chin length and she wore a bright red sundress from The House of Style. Ginger even gave her false eyelashes for the extra wow factor. Once again, Ginger took the microphone and said, "Thank you, Belinda. Now ladies, last, but certainly not least, I would like to introduce, Bernadette Clump!"

Bernadette peeked out from behind the curtain and it was all she could do to force herself to walk out. Never in all her days did she think it was possible to look the way she did today. The crowd was not expecting much with Bernadette as the poor thing had been living on a pig farm for twenty years. She was as thin as a string bean and just about as attractive. That was not meant as a criticism, it was just the sad truth. When the crowd witnessed Bernadette's transformation, they almost brought the house down. Bernadette received a dark brown shoulder-length wig. Broad further styled it for this occasion into a French twist with tendrils at the sides. She was wearing a black evening gown that Betty Lou chose for her. The dress was floor length and had a slit that went up to the upper thigh. The straps on the dress were made from rhinestones and Bernadette had on matching drop earrings. Betty Lou decided to give the winners dresses with a price tag of around two hundred dollars, but with Bernadette, she blew the bank. Bernie's dress would have cost some lucky lady six hundred and fifty dollars. The outcome was well worth it. Bernie looked like that old movie star, Audrey Hepburn. The crowd continued to thunder their applause. Ginger asked all the winners to come out on the stage together. By the end of the afternoon, Broad had ninety-three orders for custom wigs and Ginger realized coming in only one day a week wasn't going to cut it.

At four o'clock, Willy and Tommy changed out of their last costumes and put on their regular clothes. As they were getting ready to leave the third floor, they noticed two wig boxes with their names on them. Willy opened hers first. Inside was a stunning wig in her hair color that had a lovely soft curl to it. It was the exact style she was hoping for when Charlie put her hair in rollers all those weeks ago. Willy put the wig on and almost started to cry. She loved it. She saw a note pinned to the top of the box, it said:

I bet Jamie Armstrong will love this!
Love,
Athena

Tommy opened her box and found that her wig was just like the one Athena cut for Tiffany. Her note read:

Tiffany no longer deserves her own style, enjoy!
Love,
Athena

Both girls had completely forgotten that Athena had promised them wigs at the opening. This was the most amazing day ever!

Mystery Lady

Five days after the grand opening of the wig factory, everyone was still riding high on the excitement. Broad spent his days busily taking measurements for custom wig orders. Mrs. C. spent her days making cookies and talking with customers and Willy and Tommy ran the coffee bar. They were all very content. When Willy and Tommy went to the kitchen to get more cookies, they ran right smack into Bella, Aurelia and Athena. They were very excited to see them. It had been days and they were starting to wonder if their other-worldly friends left after the opening. They thanked Athena for the lovely wigs and told them all how much fun they were having.

Bella declared, "I'm so glad, dears. The three of us couldn't be more delighted with how well everything is going."

Willy announced, "Tommy and I thought you left.

We were wondering if we'd see you again."

"Well, dear, we can't stay forever, that's certainly true. But we have one more mission to take care of before we go."

Willy asked, "You mean the carousel? We were wondering when we'd hear more about that."

Tommy added, "Yeah, we've been hanging out over there in hopes of seeing Bobby, but he hasn't been around."

Bella responded, "He'll be back soon, don't worry. He has some wonderful ideas about how to get the carousel running again, too."

Willy asked, "Well, if the carousel isn't your other mission, what is?"

Bella replied, "Did you forget that we needed to get the factory opened before the thirtieth?"

Willy looked surprised, "We did! You said something about a very important lady needing our help."

"That's right Willy. As it turns out, today is the day she will require the factory's assistance."

Tommy gasped, "Today? When, today?"

Just then, they heard the bell ring over the front door. Willy and Tommy were excited to see who their mystery guest was and sped to the front room to see. It turned out to be a short, rather heavy-set lady they didn't recognize at all. The lady stood in the front room, looking around expectantly. Aunt Georgie approached her and asked if she might help her in any way.

The mystery lady asked, "Is this the wig factory? It looks more like a coffee shop."

"Actually," Aunt Georgie replied, "this is the coffee bar. The wigs are in the back in The Annex."

The lady exclaimed, "Oh, thank goodness! Is there somewhere private where you might be able to help someone out?"

"Of course dear, we could take you to the third floor. There are no customers up there."

Aunt Georgie wondered what this was all about. When the lady asked, "Is there another entrance that isn't so public?"

Aunt Georgie, Willy and Tommy looked at her like she was nuts. Why would she need a private entrance? She was already standing there. But always the diplomat, Aunt Georgie said, "Of course, you could always come through the kitchen, if you prefer. No one uses that entrance and the only buildings surrounding it are garages. No one would see you, if that's what's worrying you."

The lady was relieved to hear that. She said what she was looking for were two custom wigs. Unfortunately, she needed them by early the following morning.

Aunt Georgie said, "Dear, we would love to help you but we have ninety-three orders for custom wigs that came before yours and my policy has always been first come, first serve."

The lady was shocked by the number of custom orders this factory had. How could a wig factory in a small town in the middle of Oregon have so many orders for custom wigs?

"Oh my goodness. I am in so much trouble if I can't get those wigs. I have made the most enormous mistake and if I don't get them, well, I just can't tell you."

With that, she burst into tears. Not delicate little sobs, but great big tears. She cried and blubbered and no amount of consoling on Aunt Georgie's part was comforting her. Finally, Aunt Georgie broke down and said, "Now, now, if it's that much of a problem, we'll take care of you, but only if my staff is willing to work into the night. You must let me check with them, okay?"

The mystery woman's tears dried up a little and she reached into her purse. She handed Aunt Georgie a huge fist full of money and said, "There's fifteen hundred dollars here. I will pay extra for the wigs. I just need them by nine a.m. and I need the staff's absolute discretion. They can't speak about this to anyone outside the factory."

This was more confusing than ever. Who was this lady and what could be causing her such distress? Why did she need two custom wigs by the morning and why was she willing to pay so much money for something they wouldn't dream of charging extra for? Discretion was always free. It was just good breeding.

The lady asked Aunt Georgie if she could come back at six p.m. for the fittings after all the other customers had long gone. Aunt Georgie said that would be fine. She would wait for her in the kitchen. With that, the mystery lady left.

Unveiled

At exactly six o'clock, Willy, Tommy, and Aunt Georgie sat in the kitchen sipping cups of hot chocolate. They were all feeling great anticipation at the strange lady's return. Then at three minutes after six, there was a soft knock on the door. Aunt Georgie answered and there she was. She nervously asked, "Is anyone else around?"

Aunt Georgie assured her the only people left in the factory worked there. The lady introduced herself as Caroline DeGall. Aunt Georgie introduced herself and both Willy and Tommy.

After all the greetings were exchanged, Caroline announced, "I don't mean to be a problem Mrs. Carbunkle, but are you sure the other doors to the building are locked? I wouldn't want anyone else to inadvertently see anything."

Aunt Georgie assured Caroline the doors were all locked and she had even taken the precautions of drawing the drapes. Caroline was greatly relieved by this information and excused herself for a moment. She went back out to her car and opened the passenger side door. A lady in a black suit stepped out. She was perfectly lovely looking with the exception of the heavy black shawl draped over her head. She was tall and slender and appeared to be in her early forties. What was going on? Caroline guided the other woman to the door and got her safely into the kitchen. She addressed her audience and said, "This lady is the reason we are all here."

From beneath the shawl, the new lady asked, "Really, Caroline, do you think this cloak and dagger stuff is necessary?" She had a lovely voice. There was a hint of Southern drawl to it and something about it was very familiar.

Caroline answered her, "I'm sorry ma'am, but I do. You would not be in this predicament without my blunder and I simply refuse to have you suffer further embarrassment."

With that, the veiled lady addressed her audience and apologized, "You must all think Caroline and I just fell off the nut-wagon. I am so sorry to inflict all of this drama on you. I think it's time I take the ridiculous scarf off my head and introduce myself like a real lady should."

With that, she took off her scarf and it was none

other than Claire O'Conner, the President of the United States! She was stunning, except half of her signature long chestnut hair was missing. She stood in front of them half bald.

Willy and Tommy almost fell over. Imagine, actually standing next to the president. Aunt Georgie's reaction was smoother than silk pie. She stepped forward, put her hand out and graciously declared, "Mrs. O'Connor, what an honor to meet you. My name is Georgianna Carbunkle and it looks like you've been having a little trouble with your hair."

Claire O'Connor fell in love with Aunt Georgie on the spot. She was overcome by her refreshing forthrightness. Not one single woman in Washington D.C. would have said a thing to her about her hair, even if she showed up like that to a White House dinner. But they would have certainly said plenty behind her back.

"Mrs. Carbunkle, let me assure you, the honor is all mine. Let me explain what happened, so you don't think I was attacked by a weed whacker. I have a terrible allergy to a chemical that is commonly put into certain shampoos and I mistakenly used one of them. What you are looking at is the unfortunate result. I just flew into Oregon last evening as I had an appearance in Portland this afternoon. But after washing my hair I decided it would be best to cancel. At any rate, I was a bit at a loss for what to do when I decided to call my old friend, Catherine Smythe-Greggor. Catherine has an aunt who lives in Montieth and she speaks very highly of your little town. I understand she even bought a dress here that she wore to an event at Buckingham Palace." The president continued, "Catherine heard all about your lovely factory from her aunt and suggested I come to you for help."

Caroline couldn't keep quiet any longer and said, "What Mrs. O'Connor isn't telling you is I was the one who bought her the wrong shampoo. I know all about her allergy and I forgot to check the ingredients. The president is the guest of honor at a diplomatic dinner tomorrow night and of course she will be expected to have hair. Mrs. Carbunkle, you see how you are saving our lives here?"

Mrs. O'Connor interrupted, "Caroline, saving lives? Aren't you being a wee bit dramatic? The worst thing that would have happened is I would have attended the dinner with a head wrap on and everyone would gossip I looked like the spy, Mata Hari."

The president had a lovely sense of humor and didn't seem to feel this was a life and death situation at all. She added, "Mrs. Carbunkle, while you may not actually be saving a life here, you are certainly providing a service for which I shall be eternally grateful."

At that point Aunt Georgie suggested everyone adjourn to the third floor where Broadwyn could start taking Mrs. O'Connor's measurements. Mrs. O'Connor and Caroline were introduced to the rest of the staff and put all of them so at ease they soon forgot she was the president of the country. While all hands were busy making wigs on the second floor, Aunt Georgie and the girls stayed on the third floor and told Mrs. O'Connor all about the opening of the factory. Willy and Tommy got a little carried away and told her all about Jamie and Tiff, too. Aunt Georgie was shocked to learn the girls played such a trick on Tiff, but when she found out how she threatened Willy at the opening, she decided she was fine with it after all.

At ten-thirty Mrs. O'Connor said it was time for her to get back to her hotel. Caroline would come the next morning and pick up the wigs. Mrs. O'Connor asked for a private moment with Aunt Georgie and said, "Mrs. Carbunkle, I can't thank you enough. Could you please give this envelope to the staff and thank them for all they've done on my behalf?"

"I would be delighted to Mrs. O'Connor. Could

you please give this envelope back to Caroline and assure her she needn't have bribed us to be discreet?"

The president smiled, "I would be delighted as well, Mrs. Carbunkle." And with that Mrs. O'Connor said goodbye to Willy, Tommy, Broad, Lawrence, Harvey, and Allysa. She promised she would spread the word about The Willamette Wig Factory back in Washington. The next morning Caroline returned for the wigs and instead of two, the staff made up four at no extra charge.

Willy and Tommy were planning to walk Aunt Georgie home and spend the night with her. Before leaving, they had to go back up to the third floor to get their backpacks. They thought everyone was working on the second floor, so they were surprised to see Harvey sitting on a sofa on the third floor.

Willy asked, "Who were you talking to Harvey? I thought I heard voices?"

Harvey stammered, "Oh, hi there girls. I wasn't talking to anyone."

Just then Bella, Aurelia and Athena showed up. Bella announced, "He was talking to us dear."

"Aunt Bella? What do you mean he was talking to you? He can see you?"

"That's right, Willy. Harvey has been what you might call our 'inside guy.' He's been enormously helpful."

The girls were stunned. They hadn't gotten to know Harvey very well since he'd been there. They thought he was nice, if not extremely shy. He didn't seem to like talking very much. Now, to find out he was the *inside guy*. This was a lot of information to absorb. Bella continued, "Maybe you can ask Harvey about it some time. I think you'll be surprised by what he tells you. But now dears, we must be off. Our mission is over and it's time for us to go back."

Willy felt her eyes fill with tears. Tommy asked, "Will we ever see you again? I mean, what if we need you?"

"If you need us dear, tell Harvey, and he'll get in touch with us. In the meantime, we will check in on you every now and again. Take care of our Georgie and thank you both for all your hard work."

Willy wondered, "But what about Bobby and the carousel?"

Bella, Aurelia and Athena just smiled in response and walked away. They were gone. Just like that. The girls looked at Harvey and wondered who he really was. They were going to miss their old adventure but they smelled new ones right around the corner. After all, they wondered:

WHO THE HECK IS HARVEY STINGLE?

Recipes from the Willamette Valley

Ginger Andretti's Snickerdoodles
Charlie's Blueberry Jello surprise
      (not for use in hair)
Aunt Georgie's Morning Glory Muffins
Mr. Jim's Cinnamon Apple Mancakes
Lady Blush Punch

Ginger Andretti's Snickerdoodles

Makes 5 Dozen:

½ cup softened butter

½ cup vegetable shortening

1 ½ cups of granulated sugar

2 eggs

1 teaspoon of pure vanilla extract

2 ¾ cups all-purpose flour

2 teaspoons of cream of tartar

1 teaspoon of baking soda

¼ teaspoon of salt

Rolling mixture:

1 Tablespoon ground cinnamon

2 Tablespoons of granulated sugar

1. Preheat oven to 350 degrees.
2. In a large bowl combine, butter, shortening, sugar, eggs and vanilla extract. Beat with an electric mixer for 2-3 minutes until combined.
3. Next add cream of tartar, baking soda and salt. Mix until combined.
4. Stir in flour until completely blended.
5. In a small bowl, combine 1 Tablespoon of ground cinnamon and 2 Tablespoons of sugar.

6. Shape dough into 1" balls then roll around the cinnamon sugar until coated.

7. Place 2" apart on an un-greased cookie sheet and bake 8-10 minutes.

The cookies will look puffy at first but will flatten out as they cool.

Ginger confessed: "I'm not proud to admit this, but the day I quit modeling, I ate 12 of these in one sitting."

Charlie's Blueberry Jello Surprise
(not for use in hair)

Serves 8-10

6 oz. of berry flavored Jello

2 cups of boiling water

½ cup cold water

1-20 oz. can of crushed pineapple

2 cups of fresh blueberries

Topping:

8 oz. of soft cream cheese (room temperature)

1 cup of sour cream

½ cup of sugar

2 teaspoons of vanilla

¾ cup of chopped walnuts

1. In a large bowl, combine Jello and boiling water. Stir until Jello is totally dissolved. This will take about 4 or 5 minutes.
2. Add ½ cup of cold water.
3. Stir in crushed pineapple and juice.
4. Stir in fresh blueberries.
5. Pour in a 13" x 9" pan and refrigerate until congealed. (This will take a couple of hours.)
6. When the Jello is set, make the topping by mixing together the cream cheese, sour cream, sugar, and

vanilla in a medium size bowl. See if your mom will help you use the electric mixer. It's much faster than doing it by hand.

7. Spread the topping over the Jello and sprinkle with chopped nuts.

Tommy adds, "I'd rather eat this than wear it in my hair."

Aunt Georgie's Morning Glory Muffins

Makes an even dozen:

2 cups of biscuit mix
¼ cup of sugar
1 egg, slightly beaten
½ cup orange juice
1 Tablespoon of vegetable oil
½ cup of orange marmalade
¾ cup of chopped pecans

Topping:
3 Tablespoons of sugar
1 Tablespoon of flour
1 teaspoon of ground cinnamon
½ teaspoon of ground nutmeg

1. Preheat the oven to 400 degrees.
2. In a large bowl combine the biscuit mix and sugar.
3. Make a well in the center.
4. Combine egg, orange juice and oil until blended, pour into the center of the biscuit mixture. Stir just until moist.
5. Stir in the marmalade and the pecans.
6. Line a muffin try with paper baking cups and fill each 2/3 full of batter.

7. In a small bowl, combine sugar, flour, cinnamon, and nutmeg.
8. Sprinkle over muffins.
9. Bake for 18 minutes or until a toothpick can be inserted in the center and comes out clean.

Aunt Georgie remembers. "My boys loved these more than any other treat I ever made for them."

Mr. Jim's Cinnamon-Apple Mancakes

Makes 12:

1¼ Cups all-purpose flour

2 tablespoons sugar

2 teaspoons baking powder

¾ teaspoon of salt

1 ½ cup of milk

1 egg, slightly beaten

3 tablespoons vegetable oil

1 teaspoon ground cinnamon

2 small cooking apples, peeled and cut into small pieces

1. In a large bowl mix flour, sugar, baking powder, cinnamon and salt.
2. Add milk, egg, and salad oil. Stir until combined.
3. Stir in apples.
4. Pour ¼ cup batter onto a heated and greased griddle. Only cooking a few pancakes at a time, heat until the batter, bubbles and the bubble burst. The edges will look dry.
5. Flip mancakes over with a pancake turner and cook until the under side is golden.
6. Serve with warmed maple syrup.

Mr. Jim is known for saying, "No job is too hard when you start the day with a tall stack of mancakes!"

Lady Blush Punch

3- parts raspberry Koolaid
1-part 7-Up
Frozen Berries

1. Combine equal parts Koolaide and 7-Up in plastic containers and refrigerate until ready to serve.
2. Serve in a punch bowl with frozen berries floating around to keep it cool.

Tiffany Petersen was heard asking, "How am I ever going to get this punch stain out of my dress?"

About the Author

Whitney Dineen spent her formative years in Chicago and the outlying areas. She lived in New York City and Los Angeles the majority of her adult life and worked as a plus-size model. Whitney currently lives in the beautiful Willamette Valley in Oregon with her husband and two daughters. They love to organic garden, raise free-range chickens and dream of opening a wig factory. Whitney loves to hear from her readers. You can contact her at WhitneyDineen.com.